Praise for *Christmas Pudding*:

"In these dark days it is a public service to
write a story which keeps the reader laughing
through 300 pages."
—*The Times Literary Supplement*.

Also by Nancy Mitford available from Carroll & Graf:

Pigeon Pie

NANCY MITFORD

CHRISTMAS PUDDING

Carroll & Graf Publishers, Inc.
New York

TO ROBERT BYRON

Published by arrangement with Literistic, Ltd

First Carroll & Graf edition 1987

Carroll & Graf Publishers, Inc.
260 Fifth Avenue
New York, NY 10001

ISBN: 0-88184-342-3

Manufactured in the United States of America

PROLOGUE

Four o'clock on the First of November, a dark and foggy day. Sixteen characters in search of an author.

Paul Fotheringay sat in his Ebury Street lodgings looking at the presentation copies of his book, *Crazy Capers*, which had just arrived by post. He thought of the lonely evening ahead of him and wondered whether he should telephone to some of his friends, but decided that it would be of little use. They would all be doing things by now. He also thought of the wonderful energy of other people, of how they not only had the energy to do things all day but also to make arrangements and plans for these things which they did. It was as much as he could manage to do the things, he knew that he would never be able to make the plans as well. He continued sitting alone.

Walter Monteath was playing bridge with three people all much richer than himself. He was playing for more than he could afford to lose and was winning steadily.

Sally Monteath was trying on a dress for which, unless a miracle happened, she would never be able to pay. She looked very pretty in it.

Marcella Bracket was ringing up a young man and hinting, rather broadly, that he should take her out that evening.

Amabelle Fortescue was arranging her dinner table. She wondered whether to put a divorced husband next to his first wife, and decided that it would be a good plan; they always got on famously with each other now that this was no longer a necessary or even a desirable state of things.

Jerome Field slept in his office.

Miss Monteath, nameless as yet, slept in her pram.

Bobby Bobbin, at Eton, was writing a note to an older boy.

Philadelphia Bobbin sat in her mother's drawing-room

and looked at the fire. She hoped that death would prove less dull and boring than life.

Lady Bobbin tramped Gloucestershire mud and cursed the foot and mouth disease which had stopped the hunting that beautiful, open winter.

'I loved thee in life too little, I loved thee in death too well,' sang Lord Leamington Spa at a concert in aid of the Jollier Villages Movement. Later on he sang 'Fearful the death of the diver must be, and for an encore, 'Under the deodar'. Lady Leamington Spa agreed with the chairwoman of the movement that her husband had a charming voice. 'Our son is musical like his father,' she said proudly.

Squibby Almanack, the said son, sat with the three fair and slightly bald young men who were his friends at a Bach concert, in Bond Street.

Major Stanworth drove his Morris Cowley along the high road between Oxford and Cheltenham. He was on his way to the preparatory school where his little boy was having mumps rather badly.

Michael Lewes was sending out invitations for a garden party at H.B.M. Residency, Cairo. He thanked heaven several times aloud that he was leaving the diplomatic service for good at Christmas.

The Duchess of St. Neots was talking scandal with an old friend. Any single one of the things she said would have been sufficient to involve her in an action for criminal libel. Her daughter by a former marriage, Miss Héloïse Potts, was listening from an alcove where she very much hoped to remain undiscovered.

Sixteen characters in search of an author.

1

There is a certain room in the Tate Gallery which, in these unregenerate days, is used more as a passage-way towards the French pictures collected by Sir Joseph Duveen than as an objective in itself. There must be many lovers of painting who have hurried through it countless times and who would be unable to name or even to describe a single one of the flowerings of Victorian culture which hang there, so thoroughly does the human mind reject those impressions for which it has no use.

Indeed Paul Fotheringay, until, on the second day of November, he found himself sitting in this room, had been unaware of its very existence. He now observed that it was mostly hung with large and unpleasant works of the 'Every picture tells a story' school, interspersed with some rather inferior examples of pre-Raphaelitism and a few careful drawings by Ruskin. He sat on a hard and shiny bench and gave himself up to the contemplation of an elderly lady who was struggling, with but little success, to reproduce the handsome but unprepossessing features of Mrs. Rossetti. For it was copying day in the Tate. Paul wondered how she managed to keep the paint so beautifully smooth. He thought it very clever of her. Whenever he had tried to express himself on canvas, the result had invariably been a mass of dirty bumps; his own particular style of course, and, he liked to think, a not unpleasing one. Nevertheless, he was perfectly aware that even if he wished to do so he was incapable of producing that oleographic smoothness which seemed to come so easily to the elderly copyist.

Soon, however, his thoughts left the exterior world and turned upon his own inward wretchedness. When a man is harassed beyond endurance through the two most important aspects of life; when the labour of months bears a bitterer fruit than that of failure; and when, at the very same moment, she whom he adores shows herself once and for all unworthy of adoration; then indeed is that man unhappy.

So thought Paul; and writhing beneath the duplicated gaze of Mrs. Rossetti he considered for the hundredth time the two causes of his present depression, namely, the behaviour of his fiancée, Marcella Bracket, and the reception by the public of his first novel, *Crazy Capers*, which had been published that week. It would be difficult to say which was the more wounding. The reception accorded to his novel, indeed, appeared at first sight to have been extremely gratifying. The critics, even those of them who had been neither at Eton nor at Oxford with him, had praised it extravagantly, and with a startling unanimity; the cheque which he would eventually receive from his publisher promised to be a great deal larger than those which must so often (and so fortunately) prevent young authors from ever again putting pen to paper. The book, in fact, was an undoubted success. Nevertheless how could praise or promise of glittering gain compensate in any way to the unhappy Paul for the fact that his book, the child of his soul upon which he had expended over a year of labour, pouring forth into it all the bitterness of a bitter nature; describing earnestly, as he thought, and with passion, the subtle shades of a young man's psychology, and rising to what seemed to him an almost unbearably tragic climax with the suicide pact of his hero and heroine, had been hailed with delight on every hand as the funniest, most roaringly farcical piece of work published for years. He who had written with one goal always before him, sincere approbation from the very few, the exquisitely cultured, was now to be held up as a clown and buffoon to jeers and senseless laughter from the mob.

His eyes, fixed upon Lizzie's face, filled with tears, so that her features became blurred and her hair more woolly than ever, as he recalled with a sinking heart that one critic after another had described him as the new humorist and his book as the funniest of the month. Sadly he drew from his pocket a sheaf of press cuttings. He knew them by heart already, and to look at them again was like pressing upon the tooth that aches in the hope that after all it perhaps does not ache unbearably.

Really Funny Book by New Writer

A welcome contrast to the unrelieved gloom of Miss Lion's *Tragedy in a Farmyard* is provided by Paul Fotheringay, whose first novel, *Crazy Capers*, is the most amusing piece of work to be published for many months. This delicious whimsy maintains a high level of humour throughout, and should certainly find its way to the bookshelves of those who enjoy a quiet chuckle.

Amusing First Novel

. . . I myself paid Mr. Fotheringay the very sincere tribute of laughing out loud several times over the absurd adventures of his hero, Leander Belmont. . . . If *Crazy Capers* bears little or no relation to the experiences of actual life, one cannot but be grateful to its author for such a witty fantasy.

Ex-Undergraduate's Début as Humorist

Paul Fotheringay's first novel, *Crazy Capers* (Fodder & Shuttle-cock, 7s 6d.) is one of the most entertaining books which it has ever been my good fortune as a reviewer to read. It reminded me sometimes of Mr. Wodehouse at his funniest, and sometimes of Mr. Evelyn Waugh at his most cynical, and yet it had striking originality. I could scarcely put it down, and intend to re-read it at the earliest opportunity. *Crazy Capers* is the story of a penniless young aristocrat, Lord Leander Belmont, who on leaving Oxford with a double first is unable to find any career more suited to his abilities than that of a pawnbroker's assistant. . . . Lord Leander is an intensely funny character, and so is his fiancée, Clara. The last chapter, in which they attempt to commit suicide by drowning themselves in the Thames, but are unable, owing to the vigilance of the river police, to achieve anything more tragic than a mud bath, is in particular a masterpiece of humour. I laughed until I was literally driven from the room. . . .

With great bitterness Paul remembered how he had written that last chapter, working through the night until he felt that he had arrived at that exact blend of tragedy and pathos for which he searched. As he wrote, the tears had poured down his cheeks. The frustration of two souls, battered beyond endurance by circumstances over which they had no control, unable even to make good their escape from a world which now held nothing for them, had seemed to him a noble, beautiful and touching theme. And nobody else had even remotely apprehended his meaning, not one person.

Putting the press cuttings back into his pocket he pulled out of it a letter which turned his thoughts towards an even more painful subject.

'PAUL DARLING (it ran),

'How sweet of you to send me a copy of *Crazy Capers*—I was perfectly thrilled at the dedication, it was indeed a lovely surprise. I hope it will be a wild success, it certainly deserves to be, personally I couldn't have thought it funnier. I roared with laughter from beginning to end. I never knew you were capable of writing such a funny book. Must fly now, my sweet, as I'm going out with Eddie, so all my love and lots of kisses from

'MARCELLA.

'P.S.—See you sometime soon.'

Paul sighed deeply. That the girl whom he so distractedly adored had thus mocked his book was a wound indeed, but not a death blow; he had never, if the truth be told, entertained a very high regard for her mind. It was her unkind and neglectful conduct towards his person that was causing him so much unhappiness.

Considering her youth (she was twenty-two), Marcella Bracket had all the worst characteristics of the lion hunter developed to an extraordinary degree. She belonged to that rare and objectionable species, the intellectual snob devoid of intellect. Poets and painters were to her as earls and marquesses are to the ordinary snob; the summit of her ambition was to belong to what she considered a 'highbrow' set of people, to receive praise and adulation from the famous. Unfortunately for her, however, whilst knowing through her parents several earls and marquesses, she had not as yet managed to scrape even the most formal acquaintanceship with any great man of letters, nor had the only artist of merit to whom she was ever introduced been at all insistent that he should paint her portrait. Therefore, when poor Paul fell in love with her, which he did for some unaccountable reason at first sight, she saw in him a promising bottom rung to that particular ladder of social success which it was her ambition to climb. She even allowed him to think that they were unofficially engaged in order that she could go about with him, meeting his friends, nearly all of whom were people she had long wished to know, and at the same time picking up from him certain clichés and ideas that might be regarded as a passport to that society of which she hoped to become a member. In time, of course, she intended to marry some rich and colourless man so that she could settle down in Chelsea—a hostess; meanwhile it pleased and flattered her to feel herself the object of hopeless passion in one who had already a certain reputation for brilliance amongst the younger people.

Paul, who although he suspected something of this, only partly apprehended the situation, and moreover thought himself very much in love, was constantly plunged into a state of gloom and depression by her treatment of him. That very day, thinking thus to buy her company for the afternoon, he had invited her to luncheon at the Ritz, a luxury which he could ill afford. He had arrived there, admittedly a few moments late, to find that she was accompanied by the mindless body of Archibald ('Chikkie') Remnant. They were drinking champagne cocktails. When Paul appeared she hardly threw him a word, but continued to gossip with this moron for at least twenty minutes, after which 'Chikkie', having thrown out several unheeded hints that he would like an invitation to lunch, strolled away leaving Paul to pay for his cocktails. The meal which ensued gave him very little satisfaction; Marcella proved to be in her most irritating mood. In the intervals of ordering all the really expensive items on the menu, for it was one of her principles in life that the more you make people pay the more you can get out of them in the end, she chattered incessantly about her success

13

with various young men unknown to Paul. He gathered that, so far from it being her intention to spend the afternoon with him, she had planned to leave him the moment that lunch was over and go down to Heston for a flying lesson with another admirer. The feeling that he was so soon to lose her from his sight again made him cross and restless, and he was almost glad when she did finally depart in a large Bentley for her destination of loops, spins and jupiter wapities. He knew quite well that by now an aerial flirtation would be in progress, for Marcella was an inveterate flirt.

Meanwhile he had come to Millbank for consolation, only to discover, as so many must have done before him, that there is in good art a quality which demands contentment if not happiness in its observer, its very harmonies serving but to accentuate disharmonies within. On the other hand, contemplation of the second-rate, by arousing the mind to a sort of amused fury, can sometimes distract it a little. Hence Mrs. Rossetti. Paul felt, however, that his present unhappiness was too deeply seated to be much shaken, and that even time would be powerless against such a situation as his. There seemed to be no hope, no ray of comfort. The career for which he had longed from childhood, that of a writer, was evidently closed to him; he never wished again to face a chorus of praise uttered in such lack of comprehension. Nor could his affair with Marcella come to any more satisfactory conclusion, for although he loved her, he knew that he would always dislike her.

The copyist now came down from her high stool and began to pack up. Lights appeared, making the place look more dismal than before, and a little fog seemed to have penetrated, although outside the day had been clear and beautiful. Paul's thoughts returned to his present surroundings. He looked at his watch, which had stopped as usual, and decided that he would go home. Marcella might telephone, in which case he would like to be there—his landlady was bad at taking messages. He rose to his feet, and was about to wander towards the door when he noticed the unmistakable figure of Walter Monteath hurrying through the Turner room on his way, no doubt, to the French pictures. He looked round on hearing his name, and catching sight of Paul, said:

'Hullo, old boy, fancy seeing you here. I am pleased. Sally and I have just laughed ourselves ill over your book by the way; it is heavenly. Those policemen! Honestly, my sides ached. And the pawnbroker was divinely funny too. How did you think of it all? I'd give a lot to write a book like that, everyone's talking about it. Well, and where are you off to now?'

'I don't know,' said Paul, trying to look pleased at this praise. 'What are you doing? Can't we have a drink somewhere?'

'Yes let's. As a matter of fact, I'm just on my way to Amabelle's for a cocktail, so why don't you come along too. I know she wants to see you; she was asking about you only yesterday. If you don't mind waiting a moment while I have a look at the Puvis we'll go straight away. I've got a car outside; for once it's not being repaired at the works.'

Whilst Walter, who apparently was going to write an article on Puvis de Chavannes, was examining the picture of John the Baptist, Paul gazed at the large Manet and wished he were dead. He felt, however, that like the hero of his own book, he would be too cowardly and ineffective to achieve a satisfactory suicide; he was no Roman soldier to lean upon his sword.

Presently, as they drove towards Mrs. Fortescue's house in Portman Square, Walter said, shouting to make himself heard above the twitterings, groanings and squeakings of his ancient motor car:

'Sally and I met your Marcella last night; she was out with that poor mut Remnant and they joined our party later. We thought she was rather a dreary old do. Whatever do you see in her, Paul?'

'Heaven knows,' said Paul, drearily.

15

2

Amabelle Fortescue, unlike so many members of her late profession, was an intelligent, a cultured and a thoroughly nice woman. The profession itself had, in fact, been more a result of circumstances than the outcome of natural inclination. Cast alone and penniless upon the world at eighteen by the death of her father, who had been a respectable and well-known don at Oxford, she had immediately decided, with characteristic grasp of a situation, that the one of her many talents which amounted almost to genius should be that employed to earn her bread, board and lodging. Very soon after this decision was put into practice, the bread was, as it were, lost to sight beneath a substantial layer of Russian caviare; the board, changing with the fashions of years, first took to itself a lace tablecloth, then exposed a gleaming surface of polished mahogany, and finally became transformed into a piece of scrubbed and rotting oak; while the lodging, which had originally been one indeed, and on the wrong side of Campden Hill, was now a large and beautiful house in Portman Square.

Amabelle, without apparently the smallest effort, without arousing much jealousy or even causing much scandal, had risen to the top of her trade. Then just as, at an unusually early age, she was about to retire on her savings, she had married a charming, well-known and extremely eligible Member of Parliament whom she lost (respectably, through his death) some three years later. After her marriage she became one of the most popular women in London. Her past was forgiven and forgotten by all but the most prudish, and invitations to her house were accepted with equal satisfaction by pompous old and lively young.

The house itself was one of Amabelle's most valuable assets, and its decoration, calculated as it was to suit the taste of the semi-intelligent people who were her friends, showed a knowledge of human nature as rare as it was profound. What could be more subtle, for instance, than the instinct which had prompted her to hang on the walls of her drawing-room three paintings, all by Douanier Rousseau? Her guests, on coming into this room, were put at their ease by the presence of pictures, and 'modern' pictures at that, which they could recognize at first sight. Faced by the works of Seurat, of Matisse, even of Renoir, who knows but that they might hesitate, the name of the artist not rising immediately to their lips? But at the sight of those fantastic foliages, those mouthing monkeys, there could arise no doubt; even the most uncultured could murmur: 'What gorgeous Rousseaus you have here. I always think it is so wonderful that they were painted by a common customs official—abroad, of course.' And buoyed up by a feeling of intellectual adequacy, they would thereafter really enjoy themselves.

The rest of the house was just as cleverly arranged. Everything in it belonged to some category and could be labelled, there was nothing that could shock or startle. People knew without any effort what they ought to say about each picture, each article of furniture in turn. To the Victorian domes of wool flowers in the hall they cried, 'How decorative they are, and isn't it quaint how these things are coming back into fashion? I picked up such a pretty one myself at Brighton, and gave it to Sonia for a wedding present.' To the black glass bath those privileged to see it would say, 'Isn't that just too modern and amusing for words, but aren't you frightened the hot water might crack it, darling?' And to the Italian chairs and sideboards, the exquisite patina of whose years had been pickled off in deference to the modern taste for naked wood, 'How fascinating, now do tell me where you get all your lovely things?'

Amabelle's own personal charm operated in much the same way. She was clever enough only to open up, to put, as it were, on view, those portions of her mentality to which whomsoever she happened to be with could easily respond.

All her life she had before her one ambition, to be a success in the world of culture and fashion, and to this end alone her considerable talents and energy had been directed; from a child she had played to the gallery quite consciously and without much shame. If the fulfilment of this ambition brought with it the smallest degree of disappointment, she managed very successfully to conceal the fact from all but herself—herself and possibly one other, Jerome Field.

Jerome Field was Amabelle's official friend, so to speak, appointed by her to that position, and for life. Their friendship had already lasted over twenty years, and had been a most satisfactory one on both sides; for while Jerome was necessary to Amabelle's comfort and happiness, her only confidant, the one person who thoroughly understood her character and yet never questioned anything that she might do, she, supplying much of brightness and domesticity to an otherwise lonely existence, was no less indispensable to him. The fact that there had never been the smallest hint of love in their relationship (he being frankly in love with his business affairs and she with social life, and neither of them capable of any other real or lasting passion), lent it a peculiar flavour for which she at least was grateful.

On the afternoon of Paul's sad vigil at the Tate, Jerome Field took tea, as was his almost invariable custom, in the Douanier Rousseau drawing-room.

'The worst part of getting old in these days,' he said, 'seems to be that those of one's friends who are neither dead, dying nor bankrupt, are in prison. It is really most depressing, one never knows when one's own turn may not be coming. I said to my directors only to-day, "Now mind, if I go to the Old Bailey I don't intend to stand in the dock alone. I asked all of you to be directors on the distinct understanding that you know as well as I do how to add, substract and even multiply, and I count on you to be equally responsible with me for any slips that are made." That shook 'em, I can tell you, especially that fat old fool, Leamington Spa; he practically asked me how long we could expect to be at large.'

'But I do hope,' said Amabelle with some anxiety, 'that

you're not in immediate danger of arrest, are you? Do try and put it off till after Christmas anyhow.'

'Why, do you need me for something special at Christmas time?'

'Not more than usual, darling. I always need you as you know perfectly well. The thing is that I hope you'll come and stay with me for Christmas—I've taken a house in the country then.'

'Not in England?'

'Yes, in Gloucestershire, to be exact.'

'Good gracious, Amabelle!'

Jerome Field was one of those rare and satisfactory people who always play the exact part that would be expected of them. At this particular juncture it was obviously indicated that he should register a slightly offended amazement. He did so.

'The country in England, my dear. What a curious notion. Whatever could have made you think of such a thing? Do you say you have actually taken a house?'

Amabelle nodded.

'Have you seen it?'

She shook her head.

'How long have you taken it for, may one ask?'

'Two months. I signed the agreement to-day.'

'Without even seeing the house?'

'Yes, I couldn't be bothered to go all that way. The house agents seem to think it's very nice and comfortable and so on, and after all it's only for such a short time. I thought of moving in just before Christmas. The Monteaths are coming down with their baby, and naturally I want you too. I think it will be rather fun.'

'But it's such an extraordinary idea. Whatever will you do in the country for two months, at that time of year too? I'm afraid you'll be bored and wretched.'

'I don't know. After all, hundreds of people live in the country, I believe, and presumably they must occupy themselves somehow. Besides, it's patriotic not to go abroad now. I've heard you say so over and over again.'

'Abroad, yes. But there's nothing to stop you from staying

in London, which would surely be more pleasant than to traipse down to Gloucestershire in this weather.'

'You're not very encouraging, are you?'

'Where is this house, anyway?'

'It's called Mulberrie Farm, and it's in the Cotswolds, near Woodford—incidentally, it's quite near Compton Bobbin, so I shall expect to have little Bobby trotting round most days, and you know how I dote on that child. Apparently Mulberrie Farm itself is very old and lovely. I'm awfully excited about it.'

'Now why, apart from the obvious attractions of young Bobby (horrid little brat) do you choose the Cotswolds of all places? Anything more dreary in winter can hardly be conceived. I dare say that Devonshire or Dorset would have been quite pleasant, but the Cotswolds—!'

'Oh, it wasn't on Bobby's account in the least, much as I shall love having him so near. I didn't even discover that he lived there until after I had signed the lease. No, I read a book about the Cotswolds once when I was waiting for a train at Oban, I don't know why, but I bought it off a bookstall. I suppose I wanted change for a pound note. Anyhow, I read it, and apparently the Cotswolds are naked, grey hills with lush valleys and Saxon churches and Elizabethan farm houses and lonely wolds, which sound so entrancing, lonely wolds, don't you agree? In fact, if I like it as much as I know I shall, I might easily buy a house there and settle down among the lonely wolds for ever.'

Jerome snorted.

'Not cross, are you darling?'

'No, of course I'm not. But, frankly, I don't think you'll enjoy yourself much.'

'Then I can come straight back here, can't I?'

'Yes, that's true.'

'There's one other reason why I don't want to be in London at present,' said Amabelle slowly. 'Michael is coming back for good at Christmas, and I can't, I can't, face all that business over again. There are limits to one's powers of endurance, you know.'

'You managed him quite all right before,' said Jerome drily.

'I'm three years older now and more easily bored by that sort of thing. Besides, Michael makes such appalling scenes and I really don't feel quite equal to them any longer.'

'Who says you'll have to feel equal to them? May I remind you, my dear, that three years at Michael's age is a lifetime, and I should think it more than doubtful that he will still be in love with you when he gets back.'

'Oh, well, if you're merely going to be disagreeable—'

At this moment Paul and Walter were announced.

3

Amabelle got up to shake hands with them and began moving tables and chairs into different positions.

'Darlings, I couldn't be more pleased to see you.'

'Let me help with that.'

'Months and months since I saw Paul last.'

'If you'd just say where you want it put.'

'All right, I can manage. There that's perfect. Now Jerome and Walter can settle down to a game of backgammon, which I know they're longing to do, while I have a little chat with Paul. Come over here to the fire, darling, and tell me a whole lot of things I'm dying to know about. First of all, was your book really meant to be funny when you wrote it?—don't answer if you'd rather not; secondly, why did you cut me dead in the Ritz to-day; and thirdly, who was that very repellent female you were lunching with?'

'What a clever woman you are, Amabelle,' said Paul admiringly. 'It's perfectly terrifying how nothing ever escapes those tiny yellow eyes.'

'Large green in point of fact.'

'There's nobody like you—luckily. The book was intended as a horrible tragedy, the female was my fiancée, Marcella Bracket, and the reason I cut you was that if I hadn't she would certainly have insisted on being introduced and I know just how she would bore you.'

'Oh, I see. She's a bore as well as being hideous, is she? I must say, she looks it all right.'

'I think she's maddeningly beautiful.'

'She's certainly not that, poor girl. I can see that we shall have to get you out of this.'

'I wish you could, but unfortunately, I happen to be in love.'

'That won't last,' said Amabelle soothingly. 'It never does with you. As for the book, it's no good writing about the upper classes if you hope to be taken seriously. You must have noticed that by now? Station masters, my dear, station masters.'

'I know, I know. Of course, I have noticed. But you see my trouble is that I loathe station masters, like hell I do, and lighthouse keepers, too, and women with hare-lips and miners and men on barges and people in circuses; I hate them all equally. And I can't write dialect. But you must admit I had a pawnbroker in my book.'

'Yes, and such a pawnbroker—those Gibbon periods! Pawnbrokers, my dear, don't often talk like that in real life, at least, I can't imagine that they do. No wonder he was taken for a comic figure. What between your book and your young woman you seem to be in a pretty mess, poor darling.'

'I am indeed,' said Paul gloomily. He was enjoying this conversation as people can only enjoy talking about themselves.

'Though what it is you can see in her I don't know.'

'Go on saying that. Say that she's awful and hideous and stupid and unkind, you don't know what a lot of good it's doing me.'

'All right, I will, only don't cry if you can help it, there's a sweetie. I expect you'll get over her quite soon, you know; it's happened before, hasn't it? Still, of course, it must be hellish for you while it lasts, having to look at that penny bun face every day. The poor girl's certainly no oil painting.'

'Oh, I am glad to hear you talk like this, Amabelle: it's cheering me up no end. It makes things much less awful if you honestly think her plain, because perhaps one day I shall see her as you do, and then everything will be all right again.'

'Well, just you bring her round here some time and I'll tell you all about her.'

'Ha, ha, she'd bore you to death, she's the most cracking bore I've ever met.'

'Are you going to marry her?'

'No such luck, I'm not rich enough. Her mother's out to

catch a guardsman for her.' To Paul the word 'guardsman' was synonymous with millionaire. 'Besides, it's not as though she cared for me in the least. She only got engaged to me because she thinks I have some clever friends she would like to meet. She's a terrific intellectual snob among other things.'

'You seem to have her pretty well sized up, don't you?'

'Oh, she's driving me mad.'

'Now, don't cry, or I shall stop talking about you. Do you intend to start another book soon?'

'What's the good of that? I only get laughed at; I don't care to be made such a fool of again, I can tell you. It has hurt me terribly—terribly. Look at these.' He drew the press cuttings from his pocket. 'They mock at me, they make fun of my sacred feelings. It's not very nice for me, is it?'

'Poor sweet.'

'It's the most appalling disappointment, I must say. All my life I have wanted to write; I love it. Now I don't know what I am going to do. It is hell—hell!'

'I should keep off fiction, if I were you. People don't understand tragedy in these days, only sentiment; and quite frankly your book was a bit melodramatic, darling, wasn't it? Now, why don't you try your hand at something else, some different form?'

'Yes, perhaps I should.'

'Biography, for instance. I've always been told that it's very good mental exercise, and it can be quite profitable into the bargain.'

'What a nice woman you are, Amabelle,' said Paul, cheering up visibly. 'Thank goodness I came to see you. I never thought of biography, but of course that's the very thing for me. Yes, but whose? May I be your Boswell, darling?'

'I believe books are still censored in England, old boy, and I don't much fancy the idea of being burnt by the public hangman, thanks awfully, just the same. No, you choose carefully some really sympathetic character—and talking of sympathetic characters, here's darling Sally. How's the mother?'

'Very well considering,' said Sally, who looked enchanting in a seal-skin tippet. 'Pleased to see you, Paul—not so pleased to see Walter at the backgammon table again. What did you promise me, darling?'

'It's all right, darling. I'm throwing doubles the whole time to-day. There, you see, I've got old Jerome on the run again. Backgammoned, in fact. That's a sixteen game,' he said, leaning back in his chair and putting an arm round Sally's waist. 'Anyhow, my sweet, it's hardly fair to grumble, considering that that most peculiar garment you've got on now was bought entirely out of my winnings last week, eh? So go away, or you'll spoil the luck. '

'How's my goddaughter, Sally?' asked Paul.

'Good heavens, are you going to be its godfather too?' said Amabelle. 'Whatever induced you to ask him of all people, Sally? And how many godparents does that make?'

'Altogether about twelve, I think,' said Sally vaguely. 'We thought it would be silly not to ask Paul, as he is literally the only religious maniac we know.'

'I'm not a maniac,' said Paul angrily.

'Aren't you, darling? I think you are, though.'

'Just because I happen to be a Buchanite—'

'What's that you're saying?' said Amabelle; 'I never thought an old highbrow like you would admit to such a thing. I read them in trains myself when there's nobody looking.'

'I was not,' said Paul with dignity, 'referring to the novels of John Buchan, if that is what you mean. Of course I don't read them. Buchanism is the name given to a religious sect founded by Mrs. Elspeth Buchan, a Scotch and vastly superior prototype of Mrs. Eddy and Mrs. Besant. In fact, she started that fashion for the founding of religions by untitled married ladies which has since become almost universal. The last of her followers died in 1848, and I have constituted myself head of the N.B.M. (New Buchanite Movement.) As her teachings died with her followers I am able to make up the rules as I go along, which is pleasant. When's the christening, Sally?'

'Well, if the poor little sweet is still with us then we thought next Tuesday week (suit you?), but she's most awfully ill today, she keeps on making the sort of noises Walter does after a night out, you know.'

'D'you think she's likely to live or not?' said Paul. 'Because if there's any doubt perhaps I could use your telephone, Amabelle, to call up the jewellers and see if I'm in time to stop them engraving that mug. It's such an expensive sort, and I don't want it spoilt for nothing, I must say.'

'I believe she's expected to pull through. But tell me, Paul, how could you have it engraved, we haven't even decided what her name's going to be ourselves. I want Henrietta Maria and Walter wants Dora Mildred, and we don't seem to be able to strike anything we both like.'

'It's being engraved Elspeth (after Mrs. Buchan) Paula (for obvious reasons) Monteath, from her loving godfather, Paul Frederick Fotheringay.'

'Well, really, all the cheek! Walter, did you hear that?'

'Yes, I did. I'll offer you a double, Jerome. I think those names are O.K., don't you? It saves trouble if someone settles them for us, because perhaps now we shan't have to be quarrelling all day. Only I vote we use Paula, I'm not so wild about Buchanism myself.'

'Thanks, old boy, a very delicate compliment, if I may say so.'

'By the way,' said Walter, 'why Paula and not Pauline?'

'Cheaper. The thing is, you pay for engraving by the letters. I say, I do hope she lives all right, Sally.'

'So do I, you know. After all the trouble I've had, one way and another, it would be extraordinarily souring if she didn't. However, nanny and the charlady between them are battling for her life, as they say in the papers, like mad, so I expect she will. The charlady knows all about it, too, she has lost six herself.'

'Sounds a bit of a Jonah to me, but I don't want to depress you. Anyway, I hope you won't be sparing expense in this matter. Remember that I didn't over the mug.'

'One of your own, I suppose, with the name taken out?'

'Not my name, that's left in, you see. I had "From his loving godmother, Eliza Stratford" (the Countess of Stratford, carriage folk) taken out. That came after my name, and they're putting the words "Elspeth Paula Monteath from her loving godfather" in front of it. Such a brainwave, don't you agree? And who thought it all out for me? Dear little Marcella, bless her heart.'

'We saw Marcella last night with that man Chikkie. She's a nasty piece of work, if you like. Walter finds her so repellent that he says he can only suppose he must really be in love with her.'

'I expect he is, too. Did you ask her to be Paula's godmother?'

'No, I did not.'

'That lends her a certain distinction, doesn't it? She must be the first person in London you haven't asked.'

'How careless you Protestants are of your children's souls,' said Jerome looking up from his game. 'That poor little wretch was born months ago, and there she is, still wallowing in original sin, without mentioning the horrid risk she would run if she should die before next Tuesday week—I call it a shame. Double you, Walter. What does it feel like to be a mother, Sally?'

'Childbirth,' said Sally, 'is an unpleasing process. It must be quite awful for the father who, according to Walter, suffers even more than the mother. I don't quite understand about that, but of course I take his word for it. To be honest, I should like the baby a good deal better if she wasn't the split image of Walter's Aunt Lucy; all the same I am getting quite attached to her in a sort of way, and Walter's so impressed by being a father that he's actually looking out for a job. You know, motherhood is an enormous financial asset in these days; to begin with you get pounds and pounds for publishing a photograph of a child twice or three times her age and saying she's so well-grown because of Gatebury's food, then you get more pounds for saying that no nursing mother would care to retire without her cup of Bovo, and finally I can now edit the Mothers' and Kiddies' Sunshine Page in the *Daily Runner*

27

under my own name, so I get an extra pound a week for that. Oh, yes, the little dear is pulling her weight in the home and no mistake.'

Later that evening Paul escorted Marcella to a party given by one of her Slade friends. For Marcella, like so many girls, studied Art in her odd moments.

'It is to be a Russian party,' she told him as their taxicab threaded the mazes of S.W.14, 'in honour of Peter Dickinson, who has just come back from Moscow.'

Paul thought that under the circumstances Mr. Dickinson would most probably have preferred any other sort of party, but he refrained from saying so.

'There is to be some interesting conversation,' said Marcella.

'I hope there'll be something to drink,' said Paul.

They arrived at a basement flat decorated with tasteless frescoes. All Marcella's arty friends lived in basement flats decorated with tasteless frescoes. There were hardly any chairs, but the floor was covered with the semi-recumbent forms of dirty young men in stained and spotted grey flannel trousers and dirty young women with long greasy hair. One of the young men, presumably Peter Dickinson, was holding forth when they arrived.

'Yes, I went to see the timber camps; they are fine, wonderful, a triumph of organization. A clean, healthy outdoor life, think what that must mean to these city clerks, people accustomed only to the fetid air of offices. They are as happy as little children, and in everything that they do, their work, their play, they keep always before them their wonderful ideal of communism.'

Paul thought that they sounded rather like Boy Scouts, and was unattracted by the idea. He soon wished he could go home. Marcella had disappeared almost at once accompanied by a tall young man with side-whiskers, and he saw nobody else that he knew. Although the party was by way of being Russian he could find neither vodka, caviare nor Russian cigarettes to cheer him; in fact, the only noticeable attribute of that great country was the atmosphere of dreariness and hopeless discomfort which prevailed. The chains of love, however, kept him there until past three in the morning, when Marcella appeared and announced that she was quite ready to go home. Paul felt too tired to make a scene about the young man with side-whiskers, and devoted his remaining supply of energy to finding a taxi. These are rare in S.W.14 at three a.m.

'How all your friends do dislike me,' said Marcella complacently as they bumped away in the ancient vehicle which he had eventually procured. 'Those Monteaths were horrid to me last night. But perhaps she's jealous, poor thing, of me being so young and pretty.'

'Sally?' said Paul. 'Sally's incapable of jealousy, I assure you. Besides, she quite honestly thinks you very plain and boring indeed,' he added in an attempt at revenge for the terrible evening he had just undergone. This reply was so unexpected that Marcella was for once quite unable to defend herself, and was quiet and affectionate during the remaining part of the drive to Gloucester Square where she lived. She snuggled as close to Paul as the patent leather covering to the springless seats would allow, and in the hall of her house she gave him a long, hot and sticky kiss, saying, 'Anyhow, you think I'm beautiful, don't you?'

'The poor girl is admiration mad,' thought Paul. 'Apart from that she's not a bad little thing, though heaven knows how I can be in love with her.'

4

The more Paul considered the idea of writing a biography, the more it seemed to offer him an ideal medium for self-expression, and one into which he could pour his heart and soul without risk of ill-timed mockery. Even the most hardened and callous critic could scarcely shake his sides over the description of a deathbed scene that had really taken place. He felt that in this branch of literature lay his opportunity to establish himself as a serious writer, and to shake off the humourous reputation which he had so unwillingly acquired. Once thus established he would surely be able to publish another novel with less danger of being misunderstood. The difficulty now before him was that of finding a suitable subject; one whose work should be thoroughly sympathetic to himself and whose outlook in life should be comprehensible to him.

He considered this problem for several days, but with no result. Those people whose lives he would have enjoyed writing, notably Maria Edgeworth, Miss Austen, Elizabeth Barrett Browning and Mrs. Carlyle, seemed already to boast a formidable bibliography. Others that occurred to him, such as Dorothea Felicia Hemans, Mary Russel Mitford, and Mrs. Livingstone (the mother of Dr. Livingstone—I presume), presented almost insuperable difficulties in another direction, as little or nothing seemed to be known about them by anybody. It would be hard, in fact, to find exactly what he wanted, which was a woman of breeding, culture and some talent, living towards the last half of the nineteenth century, who was not already the subject of a 'life'.

At last, in despair of ever finding his ideal, he wandered into the London Library, where he began, in a desultory manner, to read through the opening pages of the *Dictionary of*

National Biography. Unhelpful as it appeared to be, he waded on through the Adam brothers, Prince Adolphus Frederick, Aelfred Aethling, Anerium the Welsh poet, Bishop Baggs, Praisegod Barebones, Boate de Boot, and Bertulf. Having arrived by this weary pilgrimage of the mind as far as Beorhtric, King of the West Saxons, he was just going to abandon his search for the time being when, turning over two pages at once, his eye lit upon the name Bobbin, Lady Maria.

Lady Maria Bobbin. The only wonder was that he had never thought of her before. Here, indeed, was a life worth writing, a sermon waiting to be preached. This woman, this poet, brought up amid the conventions and restrictions of the mid-Victorian era, wife of a country squire, mother of twelve children, who found time among her manifold duties to sing in noble, deathless verse such songs as 'The Redbreast's Lament', 'Prayer of a Grecian Warrior' and 'Wales in Captivity', was surely the very heroine for whom he had been searching. There was not much information about her in the *Dictionary of National Biography*, only enough to whet Paul's appetite for more, but there was an allusion to her vast correspondence and copious journals which led him to hope that these might still be extant at her home in Gloucestershire, Compton Bobbin.

In the *Dictionary of National Biography* he discovered the following bare facts of her life:

'Lady Maria Almanack, daughter of the eighth Earl of Leamington Spa, was born in 1818, and married in 1837 Sir Josiah Bobbin, M.F.H., of Compton Bobbin, Gloucestershire. From her earliest childhood she displayed an astonishing talent for writing verse, and in 1842 her parents were foolish enough to publish her "Poems" in a quarto volume. She soon recovered from the adverse criticism which these met with, and published in 1844 "Autumnal Tints", a collection of short poems including the famous "Farewell to Mount Ida". In 1845 she had her first real success with "Elegant Elegies, Tasteful Trifles and Maidenly Melodies". The following year an epic poem, the well-known "Martyrdom in Mercia", came from her pen, and after that date, in spite of her many duties as châtelaine of Compton Bobbin and mother of twelve children, she never failed to produce an annual volume, generally far from slim, of poems, ballads, sonnets, odes or romantic plays. She was, in fact, as prolific as she was gifted a writer, for, besides her published works, she found time to conduct a vast correspondence and to keep a journal which extended into 14 volumes. This treasure is now in the possession of her descendants at Compton Bobbin. During her lifetime her works enjoyed an almost world-wide popularity, and she was intimate with many of the most famous among her contemporaries, including Meredith, Carlyle, Lord Tennyson (who often spoke of the exquisite sensibility of her writing) and Queen Victoria herself. In 1896 she died from a chill which she caught at the christening of her fiftieth descendant.'

At the end of this paragraph there was no bibliography, no hint as to how or where further information was to be sought. The mention of a journal, however, was enough to spur Paul on to further action. He returned to its shelf the *Dictionary of National Biography* and had recourse instead to *Debrett's Peerage, Baronetage and Knightage*; from which he gathered that Compton Bobbin was now held by Lady Bobbin, M.F.H., J.P., in trust for her son, Sir Roderick, a minor, her husband, the late Sir Hudson Bobbin, having been drowned in the *Lusitania* disaster. Paul needed no more information. It only remained now for him to write to the present châtelaine of Compton Bobbin and ask that he might be allowed to read the journal and letters of her predecessor. In a state of excitement and enthusiasm he returned to his rooms, where he composed the following letter.

155 Ebury Street, S.W.

'Dear Madam,

'I am most anxious to write a life of the late illustrious Lady Maria Bobbin, a task which, I understand, has never yet been attempted, and one which I would devote all my energy and my poor talent to completing in a manner worthy of its subject. To do this with any degree of accuracy would however be impossible without access to those of her private papers, notably the fourteen volumes of her journal, which I assume still to be in existence at Compton Bobbin. It would be most kind and gratifying to me if you would consider lending me the said volumes—or, should you very naturally object to the idea of parting, even for a space, with documents so invaluable, perhaps you would give permission for me to reside in the local hostelry that I may study them in your house, whose atmosphere must yet I feel be redolent of Her. I would naturally work at this life in entire collaboration with yourself, submitting all proofs to you before publication.

'If I trouble you, please forgive me and remember that I do so in the interests of Art and to the perpetuation of a memory which must ever be sacred to you, to me, and to all lovers of Verse.

'Yours sincerely,
Paul Fotheringay.'

It was unfortunate that Paul, in writing this letter, had allowed himself to fall victim to the intoxication of his own style. Lady Bobbin, M.F.H., J.P., opened it together with several appeals for new hens from farmers whose old ones had been removed by Mr. Reynard. She read it over twice, found herself unfamiliar with such words as hostelry, redolent and collaboration, and handed it to her secretary, saying, 'The poor chap's batty, I suppose?' The secretary, who occasionally read book reviews, said that Paul Fotheringay was a comic writer, and would be a most unsuitable person to undertake a life of Lady Maria. She was then instructed to answer his request, as well as those of the farmers, in the negative.

Meanwhile, Paul, never doubting the success of his letter, walked on air. His fingers itched to take pen in hand, to prove once and for all to those idiotic critics that he was a serious writer; and at the same time he looked forward greatly to the perusal of Lady Maria's journal, feeling that it would provide the rarest intellectual treat. He went out and bought himself a collected edition of her works, so that he might re-read some of his favourites—'The Lament of Llywark Hen'; 'Moorish Bridal Song', 'On the Deathbed of Wallace', 'To my Brother', etc., which he did with his usual appreciation of her genius. Altogether his outlook on life became far more cheerful and optimistic than it had been before he went to see Amabelle Fortescue.

Alas, how dashed were his hopes when the letter for which he had been so eagerly waiting was found to contain the following abrupt refusal in the third person:

> 'Compton Bobbin,
>   'Compton on the Wold,
>   'Gloucestershire.

'Lady Bobbin regrets that she is unaware of the existence of any documents at Compton Bobbin which could interest Mr. Fotheringay. She cannot enter into further correspondence on this subject.'

Paul was stunned by this blow.

'And then,' he said to Amabelle, to whom he had gone immediately for consolation, 'it is so rude and horrid, I feel terribly snubbed.'

'From what I've always heard of that woman I'm not in the least surprised,' said Amabelle. 'I don't want to be governessy, darling, but I do think it was a mistake for you to write off in such a very violent hurry. It would have been more sensible to find out what sort of person she was first, and what was likely to be the best method of approach.'

'Yes, I see that now. But I was so excited when I thought of the journal in fourteen volumes that my one idea was to get hold of it as soon as I possibly could.'

'It's a pity you didn't consult me, you know. Little Bobby Bobbin (Sir Roderick) is a great buddy of mine, and I'm sure he could have fixed it for you easily. After all, the journal belongs to him, doesn't it?'

'You don't think he could smuggle it out of the house for me?'

'He'd never dare to now, it wouldn't be safe. You see, Lady Bobbin is in a very strong position as far as he is concerned because she has every penny of the money, and he's terrified of getting into her bad books. She was a great heiress, a Miss Swallowfield (tea), and if old Hudson Bobbin hadn't married

34

her the place would have gone long ago, I believe. But surely you know Bobby, don't you? Why didn't *you* ask him about it?'

'D'you mean that comic child from Eton who's always here? Of course I know him quite well, but how could I have guessed his other name was Bobbin? It's unnatural, Bobby Bobbin. Oh, dear, I do feel wretched.'

'Poor old boy, it is boring for you.'

'It's far worse than boring,' said Paul vehemently, 'it's the end of my literary career. From now onwards I am condemned to the life of a social parasite. If I can't write the life of Lady Maria I shall never set pen to paper again. She is not only my favourite poetess, but my affinity, my period, my ideal heroine. I understand her mentality, I could write the most beautiful life of her. Oh, it is too hard to bear. I tell you that since I had this idea I have thought of nothing else night and day, not even of Marcella. However, I can't despair yet, it means too much to me. I shall get inside Compton Bobbin by hook or by crook, even if I have to disguise myself as a housemaid to do it.'

Amabelle looked at him thoughtfully. There was nothing in the world she enjoyed so much as getting herself involved in other people's affairs, and she was beginning to see here a good chance to indulge in this hobby.

'Are you quite serious, Paul?'

'Yes, Amabelle. More serious than you would believe. I honestly think I could write a first-class book on Lady Maria, and I want to do it more than I've ever wanted anything.'

'Really and truly?'

'I promise you.'

'In that case, my dear, and especially if it's going to cure you of that dreary little Marcella, I think I must try to help you. I'll go down to Eton at once and call on Bobby, I expect that between us we could think out some scheme for getting you into Compton Bobbin.'

'Oh, Amabelle, if only you could,' said Paul, but he went away feeling depressed and not very hopeful.

The next day, at one o'clock punctually, Amabelle, dressed

in pale beige furs, stepped out of her pale beige Rolls-Royce into the High Street of Eton, where she was met with noisy acclamations of delight by Sir Roderick Bobbin, Baronet, of Compton Bobbin, in the county of Gloucestershire.

'Cad, cad, Amabelle darling! First of all you haven't written to me once as you promised you would, and then you send me a wire only this morning to say you're coming down. If you had let me know a tiny bit sooner I could have ordered a decent lunch, but as it is I don't know what we shall get, something uneatable probably. Two days' notice in future, please, my sweet!'

'I'm sorry, duckie, I simply couldn't. I only had to-day free, and I must see you about something very particular. I'm sure the luncheon will be perfect, anyway, it always is. In here?'

She followed Bobby into a little old house that was half curiosity shop, half restaurant. It was stuffed so full of antiques that every step had to be taken carefully for fear of knocking down some fragile object, while interspersed among the curios were luncheon tables covered with check cloths and arty crafty earthenware. Bobby passed these by, however, and led the way up a dark and narrow staircase, hung with Indian fabrics, to a miniature room at the top of the house, where luncheon for two was laid out in front of a lattice window. A peat fire burned in the open hearth, giving off a delicious smell. The room was cosy and comfortable in the extreme, and seemed to have the very definite atmosphere, unexpected in a shop, of belonging to one particular person. This was indeed the case. Sir Roderick (who had been born with an unerring instinct for living in the greatest available comfort, and who always seemed to know exactly how that comfort could be obtained with the least amount of trouble to himself) had, by dint of showering boyish charm upon the proprietress of the shop, appropriated this room to his own use, and the objects that were strewn about it in casual disorder belonged to him.

A guitar, that he could not play (lying beside a red leather gramophone that he could and did), a tasteful edition of *A la Recherche du Temps Perdu*, the complete works of Messrs.

Ronald Firbank and Aldous Huxley, together with reproductions of two of Picasso's better-known aquarelles, bore testimony to the fact that young Sir Roderick liked to associate himself with modern culture. The possessor of keen eyes, however, observing some well used bridge markers, the masterpieces of Wallace, and a positive heap of social weekly journals, might suspect that the child was in no real danger at present of overtaxing his mind.

Amabelle, who had had many opportunitites of drawing her own conclusions on these matters, sat down at the table and picked up an enormous bunch of orchids that lay beside her plate. 'Are these for me? Thank you, darling, so much.' During the excellent luncheon that followed Bobby chattered incessantly, telling her with immense gusto the latest scandals from London as viewed at Eton, generally through the prejudiced eyes of son or brother to the person concerned.

'By the way, Felton's sister, the pretty one, has run away with her chauffeur—did you know?'

'Barbara Casement? Really, darling, do be careful what you say; it sounds most unlikely to me. Are you quite certain?'

'Oh, yes, rather. Felton and I saw them driving through Slough together the day before yesterday. We rocked with laughter, I must say.'

'Well, people generally do drive with their chauffeurs, it's quite usual.'

'No, I promise it's true. Felton says she never could resist a peaked cap.'

'I can't believe it—those lovely babies, she couldn't leave them.'

'Oh, heavens,' said Bobby, suddenly whispering. 'The most awful thing—I quite forgot. Felton's people are down to-day and they're certain to be lunching in the next room. You can hear every word. Gosh, that's just about torn it.'

'We don't hear them, though.'

'I know. They never speak, that's why. But people always hear their own name, don't they? Isn't it too ghastly—what can we do?'

'Pretend I've got a dog here called Melton.'

'Oh, what a good idea. Lie down, Melton,' he shouted. 'Stop eating my bootlaces, you little devil. There, good boy, Melton—want a drinkie water?' He made loud noises intending to imitate a dog drinking until, overcome with hysteria, he and Amabelle were forced to bury their heads in cushions to smother the sound of their giggles. Presently they ascertained from the waitress, greatly to their mutual relief, that Sir Oswald and Lady Felton and their family had left about half an hour previously.

When the bill came, Bobby said, 'You can pay that, darling, if you'd like to. I don't see why I shouldn't trade on my status as a schoolboy for as long as I possibly can. All too soon I shall be the one to pay, and that will last to the end of my life, worse luck.'

'When are you leaving Eton for good?'

'I shall trail away clasping (we hope) my little leaving book and draped in my tiny Old Etonian tie at the end of the summer half, unless, of course, the beaks should happen to find out before then that you are my dentist, darling. Such bad teeth. But I don't expect they will, I'm hardly ever unlucky.'

'Is it settled what you're going to do after that?'

'Well, mother keeps on droning about Sandhurst, but I fully intend to go to Oxford, and I usually get my own way with the old girl in the end, you know, so I expect it will be all right.'

Presently they went for a walk. It was a beautiful day, sunny and windy; little golden leaves like small coins, earnest of a treasury to come, blew about the school yard; one of those days at Eton when Windsor Castle has all the appearance of the better type of Victorian water-colour painting, clean, clear and romantic. Specimens of the British aristocrat in embryo were to be seen on every hand running, or lounging about the place in and out of 'change'. They were hideous, pathetic little boys for the most part, with one feature, whether nose, ears, chin, Adam's apple or eyebrows out-stripping its fellows which, having apparently forgotten how to grow, were overshadowed quite by their monstrous neighbour. They all stared hard at Amabelle, whose beauty was of the obvious, mature description that children always admire, and looked enviously at Bobby. He was considered a bit of a masher by the younger ones; his own contemporaries, although for the most part quite fond of him, merely thought him an extremely funny joke.

As they strolled among those playing-fields whose connection with the Battle of Waterloo had been cause for so much facetious comment, Amabelle said:

'How about this holiday tutor you mentioned in your last letter—has your mother engaged one yet, d'you think?'

'Not yet, thank goodness,' said Bobby sulkily. 'It is a bit hard, you know. I saw my sister, Philadelphia, last Sunday, she came over with darling Aunt Loudie, and she says that mother is still quite determined to have one who will "get me out of doors". This out of doors idea is a perfect fetish with mamma; she quite honestly believes that there is something wrong about being under a roof unless you have to be for purposes of eating or sleeping. Last summer hols were unbelievably horrible. I was made to be out of doors from dawn till dark, and then mother and Uncle Ernest used quite often to drag me out after dinner and make me lay traps for crayfish. Cruel and boring it was.'

'I shouldn't be surprised if that's why you have such a lovely complexion; you ought to be very glad you're not like all these spotty little wretches.'

'I know,' said Bobby with alluring archness. 'But you see, I was born with that, anyhow, it's one of my natural attributes. But do say you think this tutor business is the last straw; it's such a ghastly idea.'

'Yes, in a way. But supposing it was somebody you liked very much yourself?'

'My dear, have you met many tutors?'

'Somebody you knew already—Paul Fotheringay, for instance.'

'Of course that would be heaven. But I can't quite imagine it happening, can you?'

Amabelle then expounded her plot.

When she had finished speaking Bobby cried in tones of high delight: 'It's a divine idea! You mean that Paul shall come to Compton Bobbin disguised as my tutor so that he can read up the old girl's journal without mother knowing. Oh, yes, it's there all right, neatly bound in red morocco—it takes up a whole shelf of the library. I rather think there are some bags full of letters, too. How marvellous you are to think of it, darling. Oh, what heavenly fun it will be!' and Bobby vaulted over some fairly low railings and back, casting off for a moment his mask of elderly roué and slipping on that of a tiny-child-at-its-first-pantomime, another role greatly favoured by this unnatural boy. 'Only it's too awful to think you won't be there, joining in the riot.'

'Don't be too sure of that,' said Amabelle darkly.

'You're not coming too by any chance, disguised as my nanny?'

If Amabelle flinched inwardly at this remark she showed no signs of it and merely said, 'But why the disguise? As a matter of fact though I shall be in your neighbourhood then, because I've taken a little house for Christmas time which can't be very far from you—Mulberrie Farm.'

'Oh, it's not true! You haven't taken Mulberrie Farm, have you? It's only two miles from us. You *are* an angel, Amabelle. I say, though, have you seen it?'

'No, why? Is it horrible?'

'No, no,' said Bobby hastily, 'quite attractive. Very comfortable and all that. Tee-hee, though, this will ginger up the hols for me top-hole, it will. Do you really think you can persuade m'tutor to recommend Paul to mother?'

Bobby's house-master was Amabelle's first cousin and one of her greatest friends.

'I can't see why not,' said Amabelle, 'because I honestly do think that Paul will have a very good influence on you.'

'Personally I can't imagine Paul having influence over man, woman or child.'

'Anyhow, it can do no harm and may do good, as Geoffrey said when he joined the Embassy Club. And as we are here I think I might as well go in and see Maurice about it now, so good-bye, darling, try to be good, and buy yourself some sausages with that, will you?'

Amabelle, as always, had her own way, and the upshot of her visit to Eton was that Bobby's house-master, Maurice Pringle, wrote off to Lady Bobbin highly recommending one Paul Fisher as holiday tutor to her son, Roderick.

'I am not actually acquainted with this young man, but I have received from mutual friends a most glowing account of his character and attainments, and I feel certain, from what I hear, that he is in every way qualified to fill your post. I understand that he is a particularly sportsmanlike young fellow, devoted to outdoor pursuits, and at the same time (which is important), a first-class coach. Should you wish to interview him, I shall be most happy to arrange this for you. . . .'

Lady Bobbin, however, who was at that time busy hunting five days a week, did not wish to waste one of them by spending it in London, and engaged Mr. Fisher by return of post with no mention of an interview. She merely remarked in her letter that he would be expected to ride, shoot and play golf with 'the boy', as well as to coach him in whatever subjects Mr. Pringle might think advisable, and ended up by saying that Roderick would be hunting three days a week. Paul wondered with a shudder whether he would also be obliged to participate in this unnerving sport.

The five weeks which still remained before Christmas were unpleasantly strenuous ones for Paul. His mornings were spent clinging in a frenzy of fear to the back of ancient hirelings in the Row, mild, drowsy animals which were in his eyes monsters of fire and speed, savagely awaiting an opportunity to hurl him to his doom. His afternoons, less fraught with actual danger than with the horror of an almost equally distressing boredom, alternated between a shooting school at Richmond and golf lessons in Putney. By the evening he could hardly either stand or see. He regarded himself, however, as a martyr in the cause of Art, and this sustained him. Marcella, piqued by a sudden cessation of his

41

advances, was now seldom off the telephone, a state of things which would have seemed unbelievably blissful two or three weeks before. But, although he still fed her loyally at the Ritz every day, he was beginning, if the truth must be known, to find her beauty less maddening and her lack of intelligence more so than formerly.

5

Walter and Sally Monteath, accompanied by Miss Elspeth Paula Monteath, now an accredited member of the Church of England, and her nanny, travelled down to Gloucestershire by train a few days before Christmas. They had temporarily solved their always pressing money troubles by letting their flat for a few weeks, during which time they intended to live entirely at Mrs. Fortescue's expense, and by selling the ancient motor car. This had from the first proved to be more in the nature of a luxury than an economy, and latterly it had cost them endless money and bother owing to what Walter was pleased to call 'Sally's incurable habit of ploughing her way through human flesh.' Walter, while showing a greater respect for life where pedestrians were concerned, was all too much addicted to tearing mudguards, headlights and other gadgets from onrushing vehicles. In fact, the sale of the car was regarded by all their friends as an undisguised blessing, and they themselves were highly relieved to see the last of it.

'Isn't this too perfect,' said Sally as she settled herself into the corner seat of a first-class carriage. 'Now, just run along and buy me all the weekly papers, will you, darling. Oh, you have already. Thanks so much. Do you realize,' she added, opening the *Tatler* and throwing a copy of the *Sketch* over to Walter, 'that from this moment we literally shan't have to put hand to pocket for six whole weeks. It's a beautiful thought. Such a comfort too that Amabelle's taken a small house, so that there'll only be her and Jerome for Christmas presents. Yes, I got them on Monday, hankies. Quite nice and very cheap.'

'I must say I rather hope they won't retaliate with diamond links and things. D'you remember the Liberty boxes?' said Walter.

43

Two years before, Walter and Sally, then newly-married, had spent Christmas with a millionaire and his wife. On Christmas Day Sally had duly presented them with chintz handkerchief and tie boxes from Liberty, which she had chosen with some care as being suitable gifts. Slight embarrassment had been felt even by the ordinarily shameless Monteaths when they were given in return enamel waistcoat buttons, gold cigarette and vanity cases, and a handbag with a real diamond clasp.

'Oh, I'm past minding about that sort of thing now,' said Sally cheerfully. 'I'm only so thankful Elspeth Paula did well at her christening, the angel. We ought to get quite a lot for that pearl necklace, and I suppose the mugs will fetch something. I say, here's the most ghastly photo of Paul and Marcella at a night club. Do look. Aren't they exactly like deep-sea monsters! What a girl!'

They were met at Woodford station by the beige Rolls-Royce, and on the doorstep of Mulberrie Farm by Amabelle herself, exquisitely turned out in that type of garment which is considered suitable for *le sport* by dressmakers of the Rue de la Paix.

'Thank God you've come at last,' she said in her gloomiest voice. 'Darling Sally, looking so lovely, the angel. Oh, Paula! Isn't she sweet? Well, come in. You won't like it, but I can only hope you'll be amused by it, that's all.'

'My dear Amabelle,' cried Walter in tones of horror as he followed her into the hall, 'what a house!'

'Yes, you don't have to tell me that; I've been here now for a week, kindly remember. And do you know that from what the agents said I honestly thought it was going to be really old and attractive. They never stopped talking about its old-world charm, mullioned windows, oak beams and so on. Look at it—how could I have guessed it would be anything like this?'

'You just made the mistake,' said Walter soothingly, 'of confusing old world with olde worlde. You should have been more careful to find out whether or not there was an "e"; so much hangs on that one little letter. In any case, I must

44

submit, with all deference, that the very name of the house, Mulberrie Farm, ought to have aroused your worse suspicions. I never heard anything so art and craft in my life, and I bet the yokels have no idea it's called that, they probably knew it as The Grange before all these inglenooks and things were put in. You must be crackie-boo, poor sweet, to go and take a house you've never even seen.'

'Don't tease her,' said Sally. 'I think it's divinely funny; just like those Paris restaurants made for Americans that we saw on our honeymoon.'

'I think it's very beautiful, Amabelle. I didn't know so much crooked wood existed in the world. I wonder if it was the architect's wife who bored all those worm-holes in her spare time instead of knitting jumpers. Oh, I say, too, look at the way the doors open. You just pull that little string and walk in—I do call that a dainty thought. And I adore that ironwork that looks like cardboard meant to look like ironwork; a very original touch that is. Now, I think, if you don't mind me saying so, that you ought to send up to Soloman's for some rushes to strew about the floor; then, when you've hung a couple of Fortmason hams on to those hooks in the ceiling and dressed all your servants in leathern jerkins, you'll have arrived at the true atmosphere of Ye. If I think of any other homey touches I'll let you know. It's no trouble at all to me.'

'Shut up, Walter, you fool,' said Sally. 'Anyhow, I'm sure it's a very comfortable little house.'

'That's what everybody says,' wailed Amabelle. 'Personally, I could never feel comfortable in a hideous place like this. However, now we're here I suppose we must make the best of it. Sit down, angels, and you shall have some cocktails in a minute.'

Presently Walter said: 'And how d'you think you'll enjoy life in the country, Amabelle?'

'Well, it will be better now you've come, but I can't describe to you what I've suffered so far. Frankly, I doubt whether I shall be impelled to settle down here for good, which was rather my idea in taking this house, although I suppose I shall have to stay on till the end of the lease because of Jerome saying, "I told you so." The old boy was dead right, just the same.'

'Why, what's happened? You've been bored, I suppose?'

'I've nearly gone mad, that's all. Everything seems to be so queer and awful. To begin with, the lonely wolds I was so excited about are no more wolds than my hat. Ordinary fields full of mud, that's what they are. And as for their being lonely I never heard such bosh; they are covered with cows and awful staring men in filthy clothes and huge motor things which drive slowly up and down them. And in any case I think it's dangerous to go out alone here. Only yesterday I came across the bodies of two dear little rabbits which must have been killed by some lynch-maniac. It's terrifying to think there are such men wandering about. I brought the poor mites home and gave them decent burial in the garden.'

'The lynch-maniac must have been delighted when he came back for his dinner,' said Sally. She had spent her childhood in the country. Walter remarked that the amount of sadism among the lower classes was truly terrible.

'Now, listen, Sally,' went on Amabelle. 'You've lived in the country—I want you to tell me what people do all day. I simply can't find anything to occupy myself with. Your mother, for instance, what does she do?'

'Let me think now. She always seems to be extremely busy. For one thing she grows a lot of bulbs in the winter, in a dark place.'

'Don't forget to add that they always get immensely tall and thin and finally bend over like croquet hoops,' said Walter spitefully. He was not devoted to his mother-in-law.

'Be quiet. They are very pretty.'

'But that can't take up much time,' said Amabelle. 'What I want to know is how do people fill all those hours every day; there seem to be twice as many here as there are in London.'

'Mother, of course, takes a lot of exercise, walks and so on. And every morning she puts on a pair of black silk drawers

46

and a sweater and makes indelicate gestures on the lawn. That's called Building the Body Beautiful. She's mad about it.'

'And is it really beautiful—her body, I mean?' Amabelle asked with some show of interest.

'It's all right, I think. I never really look at it much. Then, of course, she does some gardening.'

'I thought of that myself, but when I got into the garden I couldn't see anything to do. There were no flowers at all, either, only some dying chrysanthemums.'

'I think flowers are so vulgar,' said Walter. 'It sounds a nice garden to me.'

'And she orders the food every morning.'

'Oh, I could never do that, the cook would give notice at once.'

'And she's district commissioner for the Girl Guides.'

'I can't quite see myself in khaki shorts,' said Amabelle. 'I think I must be resigned to playing the gramophone and gossiping. When Jerome and Bobby arrive there'll be some bridge for you, Walter. By the way, Major Stanworth is dining here to-night.'

'Who's he?'

'A sweet man, one of my neighbours. I met him in a field yesterday opening up a dead ewe to see what she died of. It was very interesting, we made great friends at once. I expect we ought really to go and have our baths; dinner is at eight-thirty.'

Major Stanworth, whose alien presence that evening Walter and Sally had rather dreaded, turned out to be a charming person. At the beginning of dinner he seemed shy and silent, but Walter presently let loose a perfect flood of conversation by saying: 'And what was the matter with the dead ewe? I gather you were having an autopsy when Amabelle came along the other day. I hope there was no suspicion of foul play?'

Major Stanworth shook his head sadly. 'Nearly as bad, I fear,' he said; 'she was suffering from a disease known as the fluke, and once that gets among our sheep it is a knockout blow to us farmers. However, as that is the only case I have had so far I must hope for the best.'

'Oh, yes, I know,' said Walter brightly; 'fluke and mouth, I've heard of that before, but I thought only foxhounds had it.'

The major looked rather surprised, and was about to speak when Sally said, 'Don't pay any attention to Walter, he's as ignorant as a bat, poor sweet. I remember quite well when one of our farmers at home was nearly ruined by the fluke; it's a horrible scourge. Something to do with the sheep's liver, isn't it?'

'The fluke,' said Major Stanworth, sipping his sherry, 'is really a small insect. It has the most curious and interesting life history—I wonder whether you would care to hear it?'

'Indeed we would,' said Walter enthusiastically. 'I always think that one half of the world knows too little of how the other half lives.'

Thus encouraged, Major Stanworth proceeded:

'The fluke begins life as a little worm. It is born into the sheep's liver and there it reaches maturity, marries, and has an inordinate number of children,' he paused impressively, '*totally* different from itself.'

'How extraordinary,' said Amabelle.

'I don't think so at all,' said Sally. 'Look at Elspeth Paula.'

'These children,' continued the major, 'are almost immediately passed out by the sheep and find their way, as soon as may be, into the lung of—the water snail. Here they in their turn marry, reach maturity, and in due course have an inordinate number of children *totally* different from themselves.'

'What a romance!' said Walter. 'And pray where are the next wedding bells to be heard?'

'In the snail's liver. The children who were born in its lung find their way to the liver, where they reach maturity, marry, and have an inordinate number of children *totally* different from themselves, who are passed out of the snail, on to a blade of grass, and so back once more into the sheep's liver.'

'Well, I do call that a tasteful roundelay,' said Walter.

Sally choked.

'Have some fish,' said Amabelle, tactfully changing the subject. 'It's very good for the brain. I have seen it reported that Lloyd George eats great quantities of fish.'

'No fish, thank you,' said the major.

'When does your little boy begin his holidays?' asked Amabelle. Major Stanworth was a widower with an only son. His wife had died the preceding year.

'Comes back to-morrow.'

'Do you go down often and see him at his school?'

'About twice a term, you know. Unsettles the boy if one goes oftener. As a matter of fact I went down last week for the annual sports, and rather a ghastly thing happened. The father of one of the boys died in the fathers' race—just collapsed, poor chap, and died. We carried him into the gymnasium—he was a stoutish cove, too—but it was no good; he was quite dead before the doctor could get at him even.'

'What an awful thing,' said Amabelle. She was arriving at an age which no longer regards death as a funny joke.

'At my private,' said Walter, 'we had a most handy little cemetery for the fathers, just behind the cricket pav. But of course, we had a fathers' three-legged race which used to finish them off in shoals. I have even known them die at the prize-giving, from shock, I suppose, if their boys got prizes.'

'Not a bad idea that about the cemetery, what?' said the major. 'I always have said "where the oak falls, there let it lie". This poor bloke was lugged off to Suffolk in a motor hearse, I believe.'

'Why *oak*, I wonder?' said Walter. 'Why not sycamore or monkey puzzle?'

Amabelle frowned at him and asked Major Stanworth whether he had been hunting that winter.

'I have been, of course, but this beastly foot and mouth has stopped us for the present. However, Lady Bobbin tells me that if there's no fresh outbreak we should be able to start again in about ten days' time, she thinks.'

'Is Lady Bobbin a good Master?'

'Foul mouthed, very foul mouthed, you know. Scares all

the young 'uns out of their wits, but she's very good with the farmers, they understand her. Do you hunt, Monteath?'

'I love it,' said Walter. 'Unfortunately, I only did it once. Before that I used to write articles in the newspapers saying that it was cruel and ought to be stopped and so on. But when I found out what jolly fun it is I gave that up in no time.'

'Oh, well done, splendid. Still, I mean to say, you couldn't really call it cruel, now, could you? Ever seen an old dog fox hunted out of covert on a fine sunny morning? Crafty old devil, he enjoys it right enough. I know he does.'

'I'm perfectly certain he doesn't,' said Walter. 'But that's not the point. The point is that *I* do, so I very soon stopped writing the articles and spent the money I got for them on a pair of topboots. But it was awful waste really, because since then I've never had another opportunity to hunt.'

'Oh, but I call that good! Now, I'll tell you what, Monteath, as soon as this something foot and mouth has stopped I'll lend you a horse. Yes, yes, it would be a pleasure—I've got more than I can ride myself as it is. And besides that I'll give you a ride in the point-to-point, if you like.'

'No, thank you,' said Sally, firmly intervening. 'I've got nicely used to being married to Walter now. There was a time when I thought the only ideal state would be that of widowhood, but now, what with the shortage of marrying men and one thing and another, I'm not at all sure about it. I believe I should miss the old boy a whole heap, you know. Besides, I need a man's help with the little one. And Walter popped his riding boots last week.'

The major winked at Walter and announced that he himself was a prominent member of the husbands' union, and would see fair play. This remark scarcely seemed, in view of his own recent widowhood, to be in the best of taste, and was received in a somewhat embarrassed silence. This he broke himself by asking Amabelle how she had enjoyed her visit to old Mrs. Cole that morning.

'Rather moderately, to tell you the truth,' said Amabelle. 'She looked so sweet and picturesque in her garden, feeding the chickens, that I simply had to go in; but poor old thing she is filthy, isn't she? However, that can't be her fault, because when I asked if I could send her anything from here she said she'd like some soap. So I sent some along at once, and I only hope she uses it.'

The major began to laugh.

'Are you sure it was soap she asked for?' he said.

'Quite sure. Yes, of course, what else could it have been?'

'How about soup?'

'Soup? Oh, no, it wasn't soup; it was soap all right, I'm certain.'

'Well, you're wrong. She asked for soup, as a matter of fact.'

'My dear! I mean my dear Major Stanworth, how awful, I sent soap.'

'Yes, I know you did. And the big joke is that the poor old soul thought that you had sent soup tablets, so she boiled one for her dinner. The story was all round the village this afternoon. Leverett, my cowman, told me.'

'Oh,' said Amabelle, in tones of deep dismay. 'Soup! Yes, I see. But I shall have to leave for London at once, shan't I? I couldn't stay on here after doing a thing like that. How awful!'

'Now, Mrs. Fortescue, don't you worry about it. I would never have told you, only I thought it was too good a joke for you to miss.'

'I quite agree,' said Walter.

'Joke!' cried Amabelle faintly.

'Besides, I've fixed it all right for you. I went round to see her and took a couple of rabbits and told her that you were a bit hard of hearing. She was as pleased as Punch.'

'Yes, but the other people in the village must think I'm such a monster.'

'Oh, no, they're all frightfully pleased. They hate old Granny Coles like fifteen different kinds of hell because in hot weather she uses the village water supply for her garden and nobody else can get any.'

'She certainly doesn't use it for any other purpose. But it is a bit embarrassing because that's the second awful thing I've done here already.'

'What's the first?'

'The parson came to call, you see, and asked me if I would give a pound towards the bier—he said they wanted if possible to collect forty pounds for it. I said I would give five pounds, and then I thought it would be polite to take a little interest, so I asked who was going to drink all that beer. What made it worse was that he thought I was trying to be funny, and he was fearfully annoyed.'

6

Compton Bobbin is one of those houses which abound in every district of rural England, and whose chief characteristic is that they cannot but give rise, on first sight, to a feeling of depression in any sensitive observer. Nevertheless, a large, square and not unhandsome building, it bears testimony, on closer acquaintance, to the fact that it has in the past been inhabited by persons of taste and culture. But these persons have been so long dead, and the evidences of their existence have been so adequately concealed by the generations which succeeded them, that their former presence in the place is something to be supposed rather than immediately perceived. Supposed, however with some degree of certainty after a sojourn, however short, with their descendants.

It must have been, for instance, a person of taste who introduced the Chinese Chippendale mirror now hanging where only housemaids can see it in the back passage, the tails and wings of its fantastic birds sadly cracked and broken, victims of the late Sir Hudson Bobbin's addiction as a child to indoor cricket. For whom, if not for a person of taste, did Fragonard paint those pastorals, now so dirty and neglected as to be little more than squares of blackened canvas, and which must be examined in the strongest light if the grace of their composition is even faintly to emerge? They hang unnoticed in dark corners of a spare dressing-room. Again, whose were the negro slave boys in black and gold wood with which the Bobbin children have for generations terrified a new governess, and who now inhabit the big lumber-room? Whose Hepplewhite chairs on which the servants place their underclothes at night? Whose the Venetian glass chandelier, ruined by electric wiring carelessly and locally performed, which hangs, draped in dust sheets, in the disused ballroom? Whose the enamelled snuff-boxes, whose the Waterford glass jumbled together with so much horrible junk in glass-fronted cupboards on the landing? And, oh! to whom belonged the Empire crown of blue diamonds and pink pearls, transformed in 1910, the year of her marriage, into the brooch, bracelet and two rings which now adorn the unpleasing bosom, wrist and fingers of Gloria the present Lady Bobbin?

Persons of taste there have been. The eighteenth century statue of Apollo, hidden quite by dowdy evergreens; the domed temple on the island in the lake; the lake itself; the rococo bridge whose curious humped shapes are only permitted to appear beneath a tangle of ivy; the walled garden with its Italian gates and sundial; the classical lay-out of trees in the park; all testify to their charming and cultured existence. And after them persons some of whose taste might, not edify perhaps, but at any rate amuse. Those who bought the gay and touching little chintzes, beaded fire-screens, Stafford pottery, Berlin wool-work, gaudy flower paintings, and many strange products of a budding Empire; those who crowned a ram's head with silver and cairngorms and set it in triumph upon the mahogany sideboard. It is sad that of their possessions only the stuffiest should remain, nothing that might amuse, much that must appal. Stained glass windows, for instance, in each clouded amber pane of which leaps fierily the ruby Bobdgin, that legendary creature half unicorn half jackal from which the family (perhaps) derives its name. The hideous furniture and stuffy curtains in the dining-room, the stamped leather chairs and table in the study, the embossed wallpaper in the passages, and—let us speak of it quickly and never think of it again—the feudal fireplace with its load of heraldry in the hall. These, characteristically enough, remain, suffering in their turn and rendered even more horrible than they would otherwise appear by modern lighting, modern arrangement, and the exile to the boxroom of their jaunty fellows so patently designed to brighten their gloomy aspect.

The châtelaine of Compton Bobbin sat, a few days before

Christmas, reading the *Morning Post* beneath the prancing Bobdgins. It was to her, or rather to the talent of her forebears in picking and packing the strongest brand of Indian tea, that the Bobdgins owed their continued existence, for it is hardly to be supposed that any alien purchaser of the house would have tolerated for long those active little creatures. Lady Bobbin was the type of woman best described by that single adjective so explicit of its own dreary meaning, 'plain'. As a girl she had been the greatest heiress of her time and even then nobody could find a happier epithet with which to describe her looks than 'handsome', and that to the loudly expressed mystification of those of her fellow débutantes whose faces were their fortunes. At forty-five she was tall and thin but heavy of movement, her fuzzy hair uncut, her muddy skin unaided by any condiment, and with a voice like the worst sort of loud-speaker, imitating and aggressive and perpetually at work. She was without any kind of grace, either mental or physical.

At twenty-four she had married Sir Hudson Bobbin, a weak but rather charming character. To those who knew her it was a perpetual mystery, not indeed that she had married at all, as, but for the packages of tea, it must have been; but that having married she should have produced children of such charm and beauty as were possessed by her son Roderick and her daughter Philadelphia. She herself, if she had ever considered their undoubted attractiveness, would have felt it to be profoundly unimportant. (Actually, in her eyes, Roderick was merely a tiresome little schoolboy and Philadelphia a pert and disagreeable girl.) She knew that every woman has in life two main duties, to marry well and to produce a son and heir; having achieved both it was of no consequence to her whether or not the marriage was a happy one or the heir a young man of looks and distinction. Except for one terrible period, when between the sinking of Sir Hudson in the *Lusitania* and the birth of Roderick, she had been submitted to the suspense of not knowing whether the child would indeed prove to be of the required male sex, she had never known much disquietude on the score of her family life. Her daughter, beyond the initial disappointment caused by her sex, had never interested her at all, her one wish in that direction being that Philadelphia should marry as quickly and as advantageously as possible. The only thing which afforded her a real and lasting satisfaction was her pack of foxhounds. These meant to her what husband, children or artistic expression may mean to other women; they were her vanity and her delight. A hard day's hunting was to her the most exquisite of joys, and when this happiness was rendered temporarily impossible by frost, flood, or, as at present, an outbreak of foot and mouth disease in the district, her bitterness of spirit would be beyond all bounds; she would be as one mourning the untimely loss of a beloved, shut up within herself and inaccessible to sympathy.

Philadelphia Bobbin balanced a few pieces of rather dreary holly on the frame of her great grandmother's portrait by W. Etty.

'And now,' she said, getting down from the chair on which she had been standing, and viewing without satisfaction the results of her handiwork, 'I suppose I had better go and meet this hellish tutor. God, how I do hate Christmas.'

'Don't speak like that, Philadelphia,' said Lady Bobbin sharply, looking up from her perusal of the *Morning Post*, a perusal which at present was a daily torture to her since it consisted entirely in reading about the good runs of other packs of hounds which, more fortunate than hers, were not haunted by the grim spectre of foot and mouth disease. 'May I ask what else you want to be doing at this particular moment? The truth is you never do a hand's turn for anybody except yourself—self, self, self with you, all day long. You ought to be very grateful to have a motor car of your own instead of making all this fuss when you are asked, occasionally, to do some little errand for me with it. Another time I will hire a car when Fred is away. I would much sooner do that than have all these complaints. And if you're going to be in such a disgustingly bad temper, I'll thank you to keep to yourself and not spoil Christmas for everybody else. It is a time which means a great deal to some of us, I may tell you.'

'Oh, all right,' said Philadelphia. 'I can't see that having a car is anything to be so grateful for, even the butcher's boy has one, you know. And I wasn't grumbling at having to take it out; I just hate meeting strangers, that's all. What on earth am I to talk to him about all the way from Woodford?'

'It's quite unnecessary for you to talk. I suggest that you should occupy yourself with driving rather more carefully than you usually do around those Hogrush corners. The man is being paid to teach your brother, not talk to you, and I may say, whilst we are on this subject, that one of the chief reasons why I engaged a tutor these holidays is that I am not anxious for you to see a great deal of Roderick just at present. He is going through a very tiresome phase indeed, quite beyond himself with all this nonsense about not caring to go into the army and so on. I only hope that this tutor (who is, I understand, a sportsmanlike young fellow) will be able to make him see sense and get him out of doors a bit. You'd better go now, or you'll be late for that train—don't forget to ask if there are any packing cases for me at the station.'

Philadelphia stumped out of the room, banging the door as loudly as she dared, dragged on an old fur coat, fetched her car from the garage, and drove at a perfectly reckless speed to Woodford Station, where she found to her further annoyance that she was a quarter of an hour too early for the train. It was a clear night after a day of drenching rain, and as she sat looking through the open window of her car at a tiny new moon surrounded by twinkling stars and listening to the distant church bells practising, no doubt, their Christmas peal, her temper gradually improved. By the time that she heard the train approaching, so far off at first that the noise it made seemed almost to come from inside her own head, she was feeling quite well disposed towards the world in general. Presently the noise of the train grew much louder, then stopped altogether, and she knew that it had arrived at the next station. At last it came puffing through the tunnel, all lights and bustle. She could see people reading or sleeping behind the misted glass of the windows, and a man, probably, she thought, the tutor, taking luggage down from the rack. There was a long pause, then as the train heaved itself, groaning and creaking, towards its destination, a porter came up to the car with two suitcases, followed by a small young man who was fumbling in his pockets, no doubt for change.

'Are you Mr. Fisher?' said Philadelphia. 'I'm Philadelphia Bobbin. How do you do?'

'Excuse me, miss,' said the porter; 'there are two large packing cases for her ladyship. Will you take them now?'

'No, thank you,' said Philadelphia. 'They can wait.'

'I'm so sorry you had all the bother of turning out on such a cold evening,' said Paul as they drove away.

'It doesn't matter in the least; I love driving. The chauffeur's wife is in hospital and he's gone to be with her, and Bobby went out after lunch to see an Eton friend who lives near here and he isn't back yet. I expect he's found some sort of gambling, bridge or backgammon. You know Bobby, do you?'

Paul wondered whether she was in the secret and decided that she was not. 'Yes, I have met him once or twice. Have you any more brothers and sisters?'

'No, thank goodness. I expect we should have had, only father was drowned, you see, just before Bobby was born. But on Christmas Eve all my aunts and uncles and cousins come for a week, with masses of children, so the house will be quite full.' She said this almost apologetically, as though she thought that Paul might otherwise feel bored.

'Nice uncles and aunts?'

'Oh, not too bad on the whole. Uncle Ernest Leamington Spa is rather a trial because he always has such jolly ideas for a Merry Yule, but nobody pays much attention to him.'

'Do you live down here always?' He looked at a face which seemed to him, in the faintly reflected headlights of an oncoming car, to fall very little short of perfect beauty.

'Yes, we do,' she said abruptly. 'Nobody knows how horrible it is to live in the country always, you might just as well be in prison. I hate the country.'

'Would you prefer London?'

'Well, I went to London once for the season; I was coming out, you know, and I can't say I enjoyed it very much, but there must be other sorts of life there that I should enjoy.'

'Why do you think that?'

'One knows certain things about oneself.'

'You ought to marry,' said Paul. 'Girls are always happier married, I believe.'

'So my mother tells me,' said Philadelphia drily. She looked at him as though she had remembered that he was a stranger and her brother's tutor, and said no more. Presently they separated, Paul to make his first entrance into Compton Bobbin and Philadelphia to put her car away in the garage.

When he saw her again in the drawing-room before dinner he thought that she was not really as beautiful as she had seemed to be at first. Her features were certainly very good, her eyes large and of a remarkably bright blue colour; but her hair, complexion and clothes were dull and looked uncared-for. This he thought might be due to the fact that she evidently had no idea of how to (as the French say) arrange herself. A London girl with far less to go upon in the way of looks would have made twice as good an effort. He decided that she had better be handed over to Amabelle's care as soon as possible.

As Bobby had not yet put in an appearance, Lady Bobbin said that they would not wait, and began dinner without him. Half-way through the meal he strolled into the dining-room in day clothes and said, 'How *are* you?' in his most affected manner to Paul, winking at him with the eye away from Lady Bobbin. 'Sorry, mother,' he added as he took his place at the head of the table.

'Is it quite necessary to be so unpunctual for meals?' inquired Lady Bobbin in her most rasping tone of voice. 'And I think I have mentioned before that I insist upon you dressing for dinner. I can remember my dear father telling me that even when he was on one of his most strenuous safaris in the African bush he *never* omitted to dress for dinner.'

'Well, but we're not in the African bush now, are we?' said Bobby with his mouth full.

There seemed to be no reply to this piece of logic. Lady Bobbin turned to Paul with an air of effusion obviously intended to accentuate her displeasure with her son and said, 'You come here at a very unlucky moment, Mr. Fisher; our hunting has been stopped by an outbreak of foot and mouth disease on the edge of my country. I am glad to say that we are allowed to hack about in this district, but of course, nothing can make up for the season being spoilt in this way, just when the weather is so beautifully open too. It is really heart-breaking. You do hunt, I fancy?'

'No, no,' said Paul, who was bent on making a good impression; 'I hack, though.'

Lady Bobbin took this to mean that the tutor had no clothes for hunting, and nodded graciously.

'And of course,' Paul went on, 'I love to see others hunt. But how rotten about the foot and mouth—so wretched for the poor cows, too.'

'What cows?'

'The ones with feet and mouths.'

'Oh, the cows,' said Lady Bobbin vaguely. 'But they're all right. The Government slaughters them at once; humanely, too. The terrible thing about it is the way it stops hunting. Of course, it's quite obvious to me that it's all done by the Bolsheviks.'

'Now, really, mother, what do you mean by that?' said Bobby impatiently.

'Florence Prague was saying only yesterday, and I am perfectly certain she is right, that the Bolsheviks are out to do anything they can which will stop hunting. They know quite well, the devils, that every kind of sport, and especially hunting, does more to put down socialism than all the speeches in the world, so, as they can't do very much with that R.S.V.P. nonsense, they go about spreading foot and mouth germs all over the countryside. I can't imagine why the Government doesn't take active steps; it's enough to make one believe that they are in the pay of these brutes themselves. Too bad, you know.'

'Never mind,' said Bobby, throwing a look of mock despair

in the direction of Paul, who sat open-mouthed at this theory; 'the great thing is that we are allowed to hack.'

'Yes, you can hack to within a radius of five miles of Woodford. Oh, I don't fancy you will want for occupation; the golf course is in excellent order, I believe. You are very fond of golf, I hear, Mr. Fisher?'

'Yes, indeed, I love nothing more than golf. In fact, I am devoted to everything in the way of open-air sports, even hiking and biking. So long as I can be out of doors, away from stuffy houses, I am perfectly happy.'

Lady Bobbin looked at him with approval. 'Then you will like the life here, Mr. Fisher. It is a pity you do not hunt, but you can ride all day; there are plenty of horses to be exercised while the foot and mouth continues.'

Bobby, who hated to be ignored by anybody, even his mother, for long, now tried to ingratiate himself by asking, very politely, if everything was quite as it should be in the village.

'I'm sorry to say that we've had a good deal of trouble lately,' she answered. 'The new parson has proved far from satisfactory, far. Very high church indeed. I should not be at all surprised to find that he is in the pay of Rome, his services are nothing but lace and smells and all that nonsense about changing clothes every now and then. In fact, I have been obliged to give up going to church here at all. It is monstrous that this living is not in our gift. Why should some Oxford college choose a parson for us? I have written to the dear bishop about it, but I fear that he is powerless to intervene.'

'I say, that's too bad,' murmured Bobby, mentally resolving that he would go to church next Sunday.

'Another thing,' continued Lady Bobbin, 'which is causing me great anxiety is this new law allowing people to marry their uncles. It is a perfect scandal, I consider. Three of our women have done it already. It is really most discouraging just when one was beginning to hope and think that morals were improving in the village at last.'

'But if it's allowed by law, surely it cannot be immoral?'

61

said Bobby, in just that reasonable tone of voice which he knew would annoy his mother most.

'It is immoral—immoral and disgusting. That sort of thing can't be made right just by passing a few laws, you know. Besides, the Church will never countenance it. The dear bishop came to lunch not long ago, and he was saying, and of course I entirely agreed with him, dear, good old man, that a measure of this kind must be the ruin of family relationships.'

'On the contrary,' said Bobby, 'I think it will ginger things up top hole. I expect that Philadelphia already begins to look on Uncle Ernest in a new and far more fascinating light, don't you, Delphie? I must say I'm looking forward to some very matey doings this Christmas.'

'Bobby!' said his mother sharply, 'you are not to talk like that. Please get on with your food; we are all waiting for you. Silly little schoolboys like you can't be expected to understand these things, but it is unnecessary and not in the least clever to make flippant remarks about them. Mr. Fisher, I am sure, will agree with me.'

'Yes, indeed I do,' said Paul fervently. 'I can't think of a single one of my aunts whom I wouldn't sooner be dead than married to.'

'That, if I may be allowed to say so, is very much beside the point, Mr. Fisher. In any case, I don't feel at all certain that aunts are allowed. I rather fancy it is uncles only. Why they want to pass such filthy laws I cannot imagine, but there, it's so like the Government. They waste their time over useless and even harmful measures of that sort, and do absolutely nothing to wipe out Bolshevism. I said as much to our member, Sir Joseph Jenkins, last time he was here, and he quite agreed with me. A very sound man, Sir Joseph,' she added, turning to Paul; 'very much interested in all questions of drainage, sanitation, and so on—in fact, I believe he is nearly always chairman of drains committees in the House.'

'Ah,' said Paul.

There was a silence. Bobby began to giggle, but was fortunately able to conceal this fact from his mother, as there was a large bowl of holly on the table between them. Paul looked self-consciously into space, wondering whether or not he should mention passing angels, and Philadelphia took a second large helping of steamed pudding with hot plum jam. Presently Lady Bobbin spoke again.

'By the way, children, I went over to see Florence Prague this afternoon. She has quite recovered from that nasty little toss she took, but poor old Sagrada strained a ligament and has had to be put down.'

Bobby and Philadelphia made suitable comments upon this piece of news, and Lady Bobbin continued:

'Florence and I had a long chat about your holidays, and we agreed that as there is to be no hunt ball this winter it would be a good idea for me to give a little dance here for you both. I had been thinking of it for some time, but I thought that perhaps it would be wrong, in view of the present crisis, to spend money on pure amusement. Florence, however, says very sensibly that so long as we have neither champagne nor a proper band there could be no great harm in it, and of course it would give an immense amount of pleasure.'

'Not, I may say, to me,' remarked Bobby sourly. 'My dear mother, I really don't know what you can be thinking of. How can you possibly have a dance without either champagne or a band?'

'Of course you can, perfectly well. There is a young man in Woodford, the butcher's son, who plays dance music very nicely; he would play all night, I am told, for thirty shillings, and I suppose even in these days everyone likes a good cider cup. The truth is, Roderick, that you are too disgustingly spoilt for words. It is perfectly sickening trying to make plans for your amusement, because one knows quite well beforehand that nothing will be right and that you will grumble unceasingly at whatever is arranged. I said so to Florence Prague this afternoon. I said: "Now, Florence, you'll see I shall get no thanks for all this from Roderick, nothing but complaints." But all the same I see no reason why, just because you happen to have these large ideas, Philadelphia and all the other young people in the neighbourhood should be deprived of their fun. I'm afraid, my boy, that you will soon find out that nowadays it's a question between taking what is offered in the way of amusement and going without it. Very few people can afford unlimited champagne, and even if they could such extravagance would be most harmful and unpatriotic, just the very sort of thing that breeds socialism in the country.'

Everyone now looked embarrassed. Bobby turned crimson with annoyance, but did not dare answer back, and Paul said, helpfully but tactlessly: 'Why not have champagne cocktails instead? They are very economical, because you need only buy the cheapest sort of champagne, to which you add a little brandy and sugar, and people do seem to like them most awfully.'

'No, Mr. Fisher, no cocktails in this house, thank you. I regard the cocktail habit as a most pernicious and disgusting one. Besides, people get rowdy enough on champagne alone, without adding brandy to it. Why, last year, at Lady Jenkins' party, the most disgraceful things happened. I actually saw that awful Hood boy, at supper, cramming a sausage down his ear, for a bet, I suppose. Perfectly revolting, we don't want that sort of behaviour at Compton Bobbin. No, we will have good British beer and cider cup, quite sufficient for young people. Nobody need be half drunk before they can enjoy themselves, or at least I should very much hope not.'

And Lady Bobbin rose with majesty to leave the dining-room. It will be noticed that during this entire meal Philadelphia Bobbin never once opened her mouth to speak. She was a silent girl.

7

After dinner it was quite kindly indicated to Paul that he was
expected to retire to the schoolroom, which he did with
alacrity, most willing to exchange the physical presence of
Gloria Lady Bobbin for the intellectual proximity of her
predecessor. He knew that the thoughtful Bobby, who
showed him the way to his appointed sanctuary, had hidden
all the fourteen volumes of Lady Maria's journal and a vast
quantity of her letters behind the schoolroom radiator; a spot
less calculated than might, perhaps, be imagined to harm the
precious documents, the central heating apparatus at Compton Bobbin never having been known to affect the tempera-
ture of the atmosphere by so much as one degree.

The moment he was alone Paul fell, with a thrill of the most
exquisite anticipation, upon his prize. The journal consisted
of large manuscript volumes handsomely bound in red
morocco. Lady Maria's handwriting was small but very
legible, and of an extreme neatness, not one correction or
erasion appearing in any of the pages that Paul looked at.
After browsing indiscriminately for a while, examining the
little water-colour drawings that were interspersed among
the text, Paul settled down to read the fifth volume, which
began with the following words:

Jan. 1st, 1878.
Another year, with its store of tribulations and sufferings, its trials
and grievous disappointments, is now before us. Thought much last
night, while listening to the New Year bells, of the Dear Dead, and
was thankful for all they will have been spared. Felt how *willingly* I
could join them should the Call come to me. As Mr. Landor has
said, so truly and so touchingly. 'I warmed both hands before the
Fire of Life, it sinks, and I am ready to depart.' Thought of Dearest

Papa and all his sufferings so patiently borne, and of the Loved Grave at Margate. Prayed for strength in the coming year that I and my Dear Ones may be able to bear everything that is in store for us. (N.B.—Must remember to tell Mrs. Craven that the beef was overdone yesterday. It makes Josiah so very sad and angry when this is the case, and I feel that it must be *quite* unnecessary.) As I write poor Ivanhoe lies at my feet. Dear faithful beast, I fear that he may not be spared to see many more New Years; how dreary, how different this house will seem without the feeble, friendly wag of his old weatherbeaten tail. . . .

Hardly had Paul read so far when Bobby came back into the room, shut the door and settled himself down by the fire in the evident anticipation of a good gossip.

'Look here, old top,' he said, 'put down great-grand-mamma for a few minutes and listen to a very natty piece of news. No, really, something too incredible is going to happen.'

'Oh, is it? What?'

'My cousin Michael Lewes is coming to stay here to-morrow for a fortnight.'

'What is there incredible about that? Your sister told me in the car that all your aunts and uncles and cousins were coming for Christmas.'

'Oh, didn't you know? Why, Michael left England three years ago and got a post in Cairo simply because of Amabelle, because she refused to marry him. She was the love of his life. He's only been home for exactly a week, and now he'll find himself in the next house to hers—you must say it's pretty odd. They're bound to meet.'

'They may not.'

'Likely tale! I shall certainly make it my business to see that they do,' he added mischievously, giving Paul the benefit of that smile with which he had already launched, as it were, a thousand ships.

'Good gracious,' said Paul suddenly, forgetting to smile back and shutting up Lady Maria's journal with a bang. 'Lord Lewes. Yes; of course I remember all about it now. I'd no idea he was any relation to you though.'

'My first cousin. Father's sisters all married well, as it happens, which leaves me quite nicely connected.'

'You're a damned little snob.'

'I know; I glory in it.'

'Oh, you do, do you? Tell me some more about your cousin though. How old is he now?'

'Michael is thirty-two or -three I suppose. Amabelle's what? Nearly forty-five should you think? He was crazy about her, I believe, begged and implored her to marry him, but the old girl had too much sense to do that. And anyway she was frightfully bored by the whole affair. I don't wonder either. Michael's awfully sweet, you know, but not exactly a hero of romance.'

'What did his people think of it?' asked Paul.

'His father and mother are both dead, you know. My mother got hold of the wrong end of the stick, as she always does, and thought that poor darling Amabelle was a scheming old tart trying to lure him into her clutches. But Michael settled the whole thing by getting another post abroad when he saw that she was determined not to marry him.'

'D'you think he'll have got over it by now?'

'Would one ever get over being in love with Amabelle?' asked Bobby sententiously. 'I doubt it. I don't imagine Michael would anyway; he took it very hard at the time; besides, he's a sentimental old thing. It's lucky you happen to be an author, Paul, my boy. This house is going to be a perfect hotbed of copy for the next week or two. Another frightfully funny thing has happened, by the way. Mamma has left cards on Amabelle. I can only suppose she has no idea it's *that* Mrs. Fortescue.'

'How d'you know she has?'

'I've been over at Mulberrie Farm the whole afternoon playing bridge with Jerome and the Monteaths.'

'Oh, so that's your Eton friend. I thought as much. How does Amabelle like the country?'

'Loathes it, of course. She's so bored that she's taken to going out farming every day with old Major Stanworth. It's frightfully funny, I must say, to hear her talking about Runner Ducks and Middle Whites. Apparently she helped to *accouche* a cow yesterday.'

'I must go over and see her to-morrow. How am I going down with your mamma?' asked Paul, rather nervously, glancing at the precious journal.

'Quite O.K. so far. She likes the look of you she told me. But for heaven's sake keep off the subject of hunting, or I know you'll put your foot in it. Oh, and by the way, she's going to talk to you about a daily programme for me this hols., so mind you arrange that we finish all the work in the morning, then we can get out after lunch and spend our afternoons at Mulberrie Farm under the pretext of riding or playing golf. D'you see the idea? I'm going back there now—you coming?'

'I don't think so, thank you. Now that I am here I'm longing to get down to the journal. It looks too entrancing. Does your mother know you're going out?'

'No, of course she doesn't, you loopy old thing. What d'you suppose? I said good night to her ages ago, and what's more I've put a lay figure in my tiny bed in case she comes to look—it's been done before. Leave this window open for me, will you?—so long, then, see you in the morning.'

He jumped out of the window, and a few moments later a car was heard starting up in the road outside. Paul continued his perusal of the journal.

Jan. 3rd, 1878.

Went out in the donkey chaise accompanied by Edward and his dear children, who are here paying us a very happy visit. We took some pudding to poor old Mrs. Skittle; she is not, I fear, likely to be with us much longer, poor old soul, and she herself reminded me of the country proverb, 'A green Christmas makes a fat churchyard.' This Christmas has certainly been the greenest that I can remember for years past, and Josiah says the same. (N.B.—The soup was not very warm at dinner last night; this must not occur again, as it makes darling Josiah very sad.)

Little Hudson, darling Edward's eldest boy, looked so very pretty to-day in his blue dress and little pink ribbon shoes. As we approached Compton Bobbin down the oak avenue I said to him, with a wave of my hand, 'This will be yours one day, my darling,' thinking it right that he should learn his responsibilities thus early in life. He looked at me earnestly for a while, clasped together his little pink hands, and said: 'Then I must be very, very good.' This reminded me so much of the dear Queen who, when first told that she was in the succession to the throne, said with charming resolution, 'I will be good.' Heaven knows that she has kept her word.

Jan. 8th, 1878.

Heard to-day from darling Edward, who left us on Tuesday in anticipation of this happy event that dearest Feodora has been brought to bed of a lovely little girl. This makes the fourth addition to their family. Heaven grant that in time they will have a quiverful. The news came by the telegraph, and as soon as I had imparted it to darling Josiah I went up to the nursery, where little Hudson, Mildred and Millicent sat at breakfast. I nodded to Mrs. Darcy, their most excellent nurse, who was made aware by this signal of the news that I had received. I then sat down next to Hudson and said: 'Darling, the storks have brought you a little sister.' 'Where?' he cried, clapping his hands in glee. 'Does mamma know?' At this remark Mrs. Darcy and I had great difficulty in keeping our countenances.

Jan. 16th, 1878.

Alas, the little daughter born last week to Feodora passed away from us on Tuesday night. This dreadful news reached me yesterday morning by the telegraph, and for the rest of the day I was too much upset to write in my journal. Poor darling Edward, and poor, poor Feo, only a mother can guess at what she must be feeling now. Edward wrote me a dear note to say that he had been able to baptize the little one, which he did with the names Mary Ursula Christian Margaret, so I am thankful to think that the beloved little remains will be able to repose in sanctified ground. He tells me that dearest Feo is still very weak and most dreadfully sad, but beautifully resigned. She is allowed to sit up for a few hours every day and occupies herself embroidering a little shroud. How inscrutable are the ways of Providence, that He should give us this dear one to add brightness to our lives for a few days, only to take her from us in so short a space. I went up to the nursery as soon as I had received the news and found, as before, the three babies sitting at breakfast. Mrs. Darcy, observing my black garments, knew the worst at once. I sat down next to baby Hudson and told him that his new sister had gone to Heaven. 'Did the storks come and fetch her away?' he asked innocently. 'No, my darling, it was the angels who took her away,' I replied.

8

The next morning after breakfast, which took place punctually at the unalluring hour of half-past eight, Lady Bobbin sent for Paul. Sleepy and rather unnerved, he found his way to her study, a room which so exactly, in every respect, resembled a man's typical smoking-room that Paul looked round for the pipe rack without which it did not seem complete. Lady Bobbin herself, dressed in a riding habit, flannel shirt and soft felt hat, looked almost human. She was one of those women who are only tidy and presentable when wearing some kind of uniform. She sat bolt upright on a hard chair and indicated another to Paul.

'I thought, Mr. Fisher,' she said, tapping her booted leg briskly with a riding whip, 'that it would be a good plan if you and I together were to arrange a kind of daily programme for Roderick to carry out during the time that you are with us. I am a great believer in strict routine for young people, especially now that they have these ridiculously long holidays, and Roderick badly needs discipline, as you will very soon find out.'

Here she paused, looked at her watch, then out of the window, and finally at Paul, as though expecting him to make some comment.

'I think you are right. He evidently does need discipline. It seems to me that he is the sort of boy who should spend a great deal of time out in the open,' said Paul, remembering Bobby's little plan for bridge parties at Mulberrie Farm. 'Plenty of exercise and fresh air would do him a world of good, both mentally and physically; nothing like it for building character, you know. In fact,' he went on, warming to his subject, 'in all the years that I have had boys in my charge I have adhered to the motto, *Mens sana in corpore sano*. I have never found a better.'

'There is no better,' said Lady Bobbin approvingly. The tutor was making an excellent impression. 'If more young people would realize that we could do away with a great deal that is bad nowadays, and especially this unhealthy modern art, I feel certain.'

'I think we could, too.'

'Some of these artists, you know (if you could call them artists, which, personally, I don't) would be different beings after a day's hunting, do them all the good in the world, take their minds off those hideous atrocities that they pretend to like. Diseased minds, that's what they've got, diseased minds in unhealthy bodies.'

'Poor wretches,' said Paul, in tones of withering contempt.

'However, that's beside the point,' said Lady Bobbin, again looking at her watch. 'Now I had very much hoped that Roderick would be getting four or five days a week with hounds these Christmas holidays, but of course the wretched foot and mouth has stopped all that for the present (although between ourselves I have an idea that, if there are no fresh outbreaks before the new year, we shall be able to carry on just as usual in January). Luckily, however, we are not prevented from hacking on the estate, so you and he will be able to help keep the hunt horses fit. Then I shall be arranging one or two shoots for him, nothing much, you know, as we have given up rearing since my husband's death, but just rough days. Besides that there is quite a nice little golf course outside Woodford, and Major Stanworth, who is farming near here, has a squash court, so as you see there will be no lack of sport for you. Now would you be so good as to cast your eye over this piece of paper on which I have written out a daily programme for Roderick, subject, of course, to your approval, Mr. Fisher.'

'Let me see, let me see,' said Paul, fixing on to his nose a pair of pince-nez through which, in fact, he could hardly see anything at all, but which he felt to be in keeping with his new character as tutor. (Amabelle had with great difficulty restrained him from making his appearance at Compton Bobbin arrayed in a platinum blonde wig, moustache and eyebrows.)

'Ah! Hum! Hem! Yes! "Breakfast at eight-thirty, work from nine to eleven, ride from eleven to one." That won't do, you know, Lady Bobbin, won't do at all, I fear. Let me see now, "luncheon at one o'clock, ride or play golf from two till four"—that's all right—"from five till seven-thirty more work or a game of squash rackets". Yes, a very excellent programme, if I may say so, but there is one thing about it which I shall be obliged to alter. We *must* have the whole morning for work.'

'Has Mr. Pringle given Roderick so much to do?'

'Yes, indeed. A very great deal. I am afraid from what Mr. Pringle tells me that Roderick is an idle, a backward boy.'

'I know he is.'

'Mr. Pringle doubts whether Roderick will pass into Sandhurst at all unless we read the whole of Horace, selections, which he has made for us, from Pliny and Virgil, the letters of Julius Caesar, the *Iliad*, most of the Greek Anthology, Gibbon's *Decline and Fall of the Roman Empire*, Burton's *Anatomy of Melancholy*, and Froude's *Essays*,' said Paul wildly, and at random. 'And besides all that he urged on me the importance of coaching Roderick thoroughly in mathematics and European history. Personally I think it seems rather a pity to pin the boy down to his lessons when he could be reaping so much benefit from fresh air and exercise, but you know what these schoolmasters are like. Besides, you must yourself be anxious for him to pass into Sandhurst, and if he is to do so with any degree of certainty we shall, I fear, be obliged to give up more time to our work than you have allowed for on this programme.'

'Very well,' said Lady Bobbin, 'I'm sure I don't wish the boy's work to suffer, and as you say, I am very anxious that he should pass for Sandhurst. And that reminds me of something I wanted to mention to you—please do all that you can to persuade Roderick that he wants to go into the army. He has an absurd idea of becoming a diplomat, which I should very much dislike. I myself am a soldier's daughter and a soldier's wife—'

'So am I,' said Paul. 'At least I am a soldier's son and my mother was a soldier's wife.'

'And I particularly wish Roderick to become a soldier, to carry on the tradition in his father's regiment, so that I shall be very much obliged to you for any influence you may bring to bear in this direction. Now tell me how you intend to arrange your day, and then I must go out.'

'I fear that it will be necessary for us to work from nine to one a.m. Personally, I am a great believer in morning work for young people. I think it most valuable. The whole afternoon will then be free for outdoor exercise—I am glad to hear that there are some squash courts near-by, as we shall be able to play them after it is too dark for riding or golf. We will see how the work is going, but I expect that I shall be obliged to call upon a couple of hours of his time after dinner as well.'

'I see that you intend to be very severe with Roderick, so much the better. The boy has needed a man's hand for some years. I'm afraid I have been rather inclined to spoil him myself. All right, then, we'll leave it at that. I should be obliged if you would let me know from time to time how the work is getting on.'

So saying, Lady Bobbin hurried away to the stables.

'That's grand,' said Bobby, when Paul had told him with a good deal of unseemly merriment, the results of his interview. 'I'm thankful you were quite firm about the morning work. Actually, of course, what I shall do is to tuck up on this sofa; it doesn't suit my constitution to be awake before lunch time, while you get on with great-grandmamma's journal. You might read out any juicy bits that you happen to come across. Then the moment lunch is finished we'll hack over to Mulberrie Farm. Amabelle says there is a groom who can exercise the horses for us, while we play bridge and gossip with her—I'll tell him to jolly well tire them out, too. If we get back late we'll pretend that we stopped at Woodford Manor (that's Major Stanworth's) for a game of squash and some tea.

Mother will be awfully pleased. Well, thanks to you, Paul, old boy, I'm looking forward to the decentest hols. for years.' And Bobby flung himself on to the sofa, where he immediately fell asleep.

Meanwhile Paul returned to the journal, and was soon in the middle of that part of it which describes at immense length and in great detail the last weeks and hours of Sir Josiah Bobbin, who died, at the age of sixty-one, evidently from chronic over-eating.

Aug. 6th, 1878.

Spent many happy hours to-day in the Beloved Sick Room. I occupied some of them by reading aloud from the 'Idylls of the King', a work combining such noble sentiments with such an interesting narrative (both of which are, in my opinion, and that of Josiah, a *sine qua non* of *really great* poetry) that it is truly pleasant and edifying to read. How different from *so much* that is written in these days! My Dear One slept most of the time. He still has, I am most thankful to say, a good appetite, although so unwell, and it is by the means of constant feeding with nourishing foods that we are able to maintain his Precious Strength. It is now very late, almost midnight, the hour always consecrated to my journal. Ah! Faithful Page, to thee how many sorrows have I confided, safe in the knowledge that thou at least will never misconstrue my meaning, never repeat my secrets to a hard, uncomprehending world. To-night I will unburden more of myself to thee, as I sit beside the Beloved Bed. For the day which is just dawning is the anniversary of the death of Dearest Mamma, who passed away when I was but an unthinking babe of four months old. Oh, cruel Fate which robbed nine little ones of their Guiding Star at such an early age, leaving them to reach maturity without a Mother's care.

At such sacred moments I sometimes think that I myself could have made a truer Wife, a more attentive Mother, if I had been less devoted to my Art. Alas! Can it be so? Would Arthur, George, Edward, Albert, Frederick and William, Alice, Julia, Maud, Eva, Louise and Beatrice have been *better* men and women, had I given up my writing? The very thought is a knife in my heart! Would darling Josiah have had a *more perfect* helpmeet but for the cultivation of my Gift? The knife turns! And yet I console myself with remembering that Nature teaches us a different, and, I hope, a truer lesson. The gentle Nightingale can ever find time for the duties of her home in

75

the intevals of charming the woodlands with her silvery note; the merry lark, soaring above the cornfields, the perky robin hopping among the evergreens, each has its little song to sing, yet is not therefore a *neglectful* Mother! And surely it has ever been thus with me? Surely I have no cause for self-reproach on that dread score? I *know* that I have not, otherwise how could I survive another moment at such a melancholy time? Sometimes it comes upon me with a fearful shudder that I am soon to be left a Widow. Widow! Hateful word, how could these fingers fashion thee? Surely I must be spared that unberable, that fatal blow awhile? And yet I saw in the doctor's eye to-day a look of cruel foreboding as he said: 'Give Sir Josiah anything he likes to eat, we must not cross him now.' That word 'now', I shuddered as I heard it, nor dared to ask its meaning.

> *Ah! Leave, my darling, leave me not awhile,*
> *Lonely upon this planet sere and grey;*
> *Spare my poor heart such melancholy trial,*
> *Lest frail my courage faint and fade away.*
>
> *Forget that thou art ill and tired of woe,*
> *Think rather of the day when first we met.*
> *Forget the hateful burdens here below,*
> *Sorrow, ingratitude and loss, forget!*
>
> *Think only, love, upon our wedding day,*
> *The lilies and the sunshine and the bells;*
> *Of how, the service o'er, we drove away*
> *To our blest honeymoon at Tunbridge Wells.*
>
> *Think of our life together all these years,*
> *The joys we've shared, the sorrows we have known;*
> *The laughter of our children, and their tears,*
> *The happiness of duty bravely done.*
>
> *But if with longing thou art overcome*
> *To leave forthwith this sad and tearful earth,*
> *E'en should my heart with poignant grief be numb,*
> *It yet would not begrudge thee Heavenly birth!*
>
> *Then song of nightingales in the wet leaves*
> *Of churchyard yews shall be thy heavy dirge;*
> *Though for a space alone my bosom heaves,*
> *It everlastingly with thine shall merge!*

Paul recognized these as being the first verses of what later became one of Lady Maria's best known and most popular poems, 'At a Husband's Death-Bed, or The Passing of a Beloved', set to music by her son-in-law, Lord Otto Pulman, and published shortly after Sir Josiah's death. Presently he came to the following entry:

Aug. 26th, 1878.

'Tis o'er. All is over, and I a Widow. Little Hudson came to me just now as I sat by the Loved Remains in a kind of sad trance.

'Granny,' he said, in his little lisping voice, 'what is a widow, granny?'

'Alas! I am a widow, my love,' I replied.

'And granny,' went on the poor innocent, 'what is a corpse granny?'

'Look there,' I said in awful tones, pointing to the Bed.

'But, granny, I want to see a corpse. That's only grandpa, gone to sleep.'

At this I quite broke down, and I think that the tears have done me some little good. Now I must collect my thoughts and try to recall, while it is yet fresh in my memory, every incident connected with The End.

At four o'clock, or it may have been a few minutes later, I went to my room, to rest before tea time. I removed some of my garments and lay down on the couch, and I think I must have dozed for a few moments. At any rate, I remember nothing more until I saw, with a *fearful start*, that darling Alice was standing near me, pointing with her hand towards Heaven. I realized, as soon as I observed this significant and awful gesture, that The End *must* now be very near, so hastily throwing a shawl around my shoulders I returned to the Bedside, where I found dear Arthur, George, Edward, Albert, Frederick, William, Julia, Maud, Eva, Louise and Beatrice standing around it in various attitudes of pious resignation very beautiful to see. As I approached my darling Josiah he turned over in bed, a smile of happy anticipation o'erspread his features and he spoke, not very coherently, a few words. In my agitation I thought at first that he was saying 'Bring me the oysters,' a dish to which he has ever been most partial, but of course, as dearest Edward remarked when speaking of it to me afterwards, he must really have said, 'Bury me in the cloisters,' a curious fancy as there are no cloisters in this neighbourhood. There was a long silence after this, which my Loved One broke himself. He looked darling Edward full in the face, said, very loudly, 'Pass the Port,' and fell lifeless to his pillow. Edward said immediately, in low but ringing tones, 'Safe past the Port indeed, Life's perilous journey done.' A moment later dearest Alice very reverently took my blue shawl from off my shoulders and replaced it with a black one. Then and only then did I realize that it was all over, and I indeed a Widow. The *best*, the *noblest* husband that woman ever had—I can write no more at present.

Aug. 31st, 1878.
I have just returned to the house from attending My Angel's funeral. Such a long, and such a very beautiful service, how he would have rejoiced in it had he but been there to participate. Afterwards I sent for Mr. Brawn, our incumbent, and spoke with him upon the subject, now most dear to my Poor Widowed Heart, that of erecting some Gothick cloisters in the churchyard as a memorial to Him. It was His dying wish. Mr. Brawn, I am thankful to say, is delighted with the idea and has made one or two very feeling suggestions. He thinks, and this shows him to be a man of true sensibility, that the cloisters should have fourteen arches, one for Darling Josiah, one for myself, and one for each of our dear sons and daughters. The Dear Tomb can then repose in the middle.

The children have been very kind and considerate, and so have the poor people, who for miles around came with their little offerings of flowers, most touching. Baby Hudson's has been the only smiling face on which I have looked for days. I would hardly have it otherwise; he is mercifully too young as yet to know the dreadful anguish which he must else have felt at the loss of Such a Grandfather.

Paul read on for the rest of that day. (It was pouring wet, and even Lady Bobbin conceded, at luncheon time, that their first ride had better be postponed until slightly more reasonable weather should have set in. Bobby and Philadelphia went instead to Oxford to do some Christmas shopping, and to bring back Lord Lewes, who had telephoned to say that his car had broken down there.)

Lady Maria Bobbin, after the death of her husband, retired to a dower house in the park, where she lived for some years with her only unmarried daughter, Eva, as a companion. Her life there appeared to have been singularly uneventful, except for certain little disagreements with her daughter-in-law, Lady Feodora Bobbin, whom she too evidently detested, until, in 1888, Paul came upon the following entry:

June 3rd, 1888.

A most extraordinary and agitating event occurred this afternoon. A person of the name of Hardysides came to see me and made a proposal for dear Eva's hand. I very naturally said that I could not possibly consider this matter, and bid him good day; but the whole affair has upset me dreadfully. Supposing that Eva were in time to marry? Not Hardysides, of course, the idea is ridiculous, but supposing (which God be thanked is unlikely owing to our very retired position) that some young man of family and fortune were to make an offer for her? What could I say? For Eva's presence here is very necessary to me. If she left me, who would copy out my poems ready for the publisher? Who would order the food, arrange the flowers, attend to the linen and perform the hundred and one little odd jobs which it is a daughter's plain and joyous duty to do for her Mother? I *cannot* believe that dearest Eva would be so *base* and *selfish* as to leave me alone for the few years that remain before I join my beloved Josiah on High. Who are these Hardysides? A family with which I seem to be unacquainted. I very much hope that *no more* will be said on the subject, as these shocks are *most* injurious to my health.

June 4th, 1888.

Dearest Eva herself broached the subject of Mr. Hardysides (whom she *most* improperly refers to by his christian name of Horace) during the time which I always devote to my correspondence. I kindly, but very firmly, explained my reasons for objecting to this marriage, *absurd, preposterous, unthinkable,* and indicated to the dear child that I should be much obliged if, in future, she would refrain from taking up my valuable time with such foolishness. I feel *quite tired* and done up, but I am thankful to think that this will not occur again. (It appears that Mr. Hardysides is an artist, an acquaintance of dearest Feodora's, and has several times lately been to stay at Compton Bobbin. I must speak to darling Edward about this.)

June 8th, 1888.

I feel so much agitated that I can hardly even hold my pen, to communicate my feelings to *this* Sacred Page. That any child of mine should behave with such ingratitude, such selfishness, such rank inconsideration for others, and such utter lack of modesty or self-restraint, is hard to record. This Little Book has been the recipient of *many* sorrows and *some* joys, but never before has it chronicled a Deed of this description. Let the facts then speak for themselves, for who am I to judge another sinner?

This morning, as I was pondering over the proofs of my 'Peasant Children on Mount Snowdon', Eva came into my morning-room, wearing as I noticed somewhat to my surprise, a new bonnet and shawl.

'Are you going out, dearest child?' I said, intending, if this should indeed prove to be the case, to give her one or two little commissions for me in the village.

'Yes, dear mamma,' she replied, a guilty flush o'er spreading (and, alas! with what reason) her usually somewhat pallid cheeks. 'I have just come to acquaint you with the fact that I am now going out to be married, by special licence, to Horace Hardysides.'

I flatter myself that I maintained, on hearing these insolent words, an admirable composure.

'Then Go!' I said, in very *awful* tones, which I fear may ring in poor Eva's ears to the hour of her death. 'Go! But do not seek to return! When your Hardysides has proved himself false and unfaithful, *this* roof shall never shelter you again!'

'Mamma!' she said, imploringly, the full sense of her guilt coming over her, no doubt, for the first time.

'Go!' I reiterated. 'Pray go!'

Hesitatingly, she turned and went.

Without another word, without even so much as a glance, she left her lonely, *Widowed* Mother for the embraces of a stranger. May *he* never use *her* so! How sharper than the serpent's tooth—

I have sent in haste for dear Edward and told him to summon dear Arthur, George, Albert, Frederick and William, Alice, Julia, Maud and Louise. (Darling Beatrice is shortly expecting a happy event, and I refused to have her informed, as I fear that the shock might have *disastrous consequences* and jeopardize a little Life.) No doubt they will all, as ever, be very kind, but ah! how I long on such occasions for the guidance and wisdom of my own Sainted Josiah—I can only hope that in a very little while we shall once more be united—Above! This Happy and Dreadful thought has made me wonder how Eva will be enabled to meet her Father's eye when her day shall come—if, indeed one so selfish and untruthful be granted entrance to the Heavenly Spheres. Poor, poor misguided Child.

Later.

My darling Edward has just been round to see me. He is very much perturbed, not only upon my account, though, naturally, I am his chief preoccupation in the matter, but also because of the disgrace which poor Eva's dreadful action will have brought upon the whole Family. Dearest Feodora is immeasurably distressed (he says) and well she may be, at her share in this matter. It appears that she met this Mr. Hardysides in London and asked him down to Compton Bobbin to paint a group of herself and the five eldest children. The picture was never finished, as darling Edward, when in Town, was taken to see some of the artist's works; and finding that they were most dreadfully secular and unedifying, besides being devoid of the smallest genius, whether of composition, style or design, and finding also that Mr. Hardysides had a most *unsavoury* and *immoral* reputation, he gave him his immediate *congé*. Since then it would appear that the wretch has been staying in the neighbourhood in order to complete his seduction—already half begun—of poor Eva. I am saddened and amazed, and can write no more for to-day.

9

Lord Lewes, who arrived that evening, was the true type of Foreign Office 'young' man. (Men remain, for some reason, 'young men' longer in the Foreign Office than in any other profession.) He was tall, very correctly dressed in a style indicating the presence of money rather than of imagination, and had a mournful, thin, eighteenth-century face. His correct and slightly pompous manner combined with the absence in his speech of such expressions as 'O.K. loo', 'I *couldn't* be more amused', 'We'll call it a day', 'lousy', 'It was a riot', 'My sweetie-boo' and 'What a poodle-pie' to indicate the barrier of half a generation between himself, Paul and Bobby; a barrier which more than any other often precludes understanding, if not friendship, between young and youngish people.

He appeared, in a totally undistinguished way, however, to be a person of some culture, and since being *en poste* at Cairo, had interested himself mainly in Egyptology. He told Paul that he had recently spent much time and money on excavations, and had been rewarded, just before he had left, by finding the tomb of some early and unknown (he did not use the word 'bogus') Shepherd King, the unearthing of which had caused a certain stir amongst Egyptologists.

'Isn't it supposed to be unlucky to dig up tombs?' asked Philadelphia, who had languidly been listening to Michael's conversation.

'Who was it said that "only shallow men believe in luck"?' he replied, smiling sadly. 'Emerson, I think. In any case, it is certain that if luck exists I have had a very small share of it in my life, either before digging up poor old Papuachnas or since. Besides, I haven't kept any of the things I found for myself, not a single scarab, and I think that might make a difference, don't you?'

82

Paul, who had a practical side to his nature, thought that he himself would easily be able to endure the kind of lucklessness that brought with it a marquisate, a superb Adam house and fifteen thousand pounds a year. He felt sure that Michael Lewes still believed that he was in love with Mrs. Fortescue; he evidently considered himself to be an unhappy person, hardly used by Fate.

'It is curious,' went on Lord Lewes, 'to consider the hold that Egyptology takes on people. Nearly everyone seems to be more or less interested in it, more so, I believe, than in any other ancient history, not excepting even that of Greece herself. The most unlikely people used to ask if they could come to see my little collection in Cairo; débutantes from London, for instance, and their mothers, people you would think had no feeling for such things.'

'It is the human interest,' said Paul. '(And I don't mean only in the case of the débutantes.) I believe that most people have felt it at one time or another. Of course, it is very romantic to think of those tombs, found exactly as they were left at the beginning of the world, full of art treasures and jewels, the pill of historical research is gilded with the primitive and universal excitement of a treasure hunt. Personally, I have always thought that as a rule it is people of more imagination than intellect who feel drawn towards Egypt. Whereas the Philhelene, for instance, is less concerned with how the Greek lived than with how he *thought*, the average Egyptologist always seems to be rather too much fascinated by the little objects of everyday life which he has found, and rather too busy reconstructing the exact uses to which they were put, to look below the surface for spiritual manifestations of the age in which they were made.'

'Perhaps on the whole you may be right,' said Lord Lewes. 'One does not, however, have to look very far for such manifestations; they are all around one in that country. The Egyptian was a superb artist.'

'Ah! But for such a short time when measured by the length of his civilization . While the art was strictly formalized, I admit that it was good, almost great. Under Aknahton—

correct me if I am wrong—the representational school came into being. After that, to my way of thinking, there was no more art in Egypt.'

'There, I am afraid, I cannot possibly agree with you,' said Lord Lewes with his charming smile. 'I must regard Aknahton and his artists as very wonderful reformers, and their art as some of the greatest that can be found anywhere in the world.'

'Yes, you see we have a different point of view. I cannot possibly admire purely representational art,' said Paul, thinking how few people there were so tolerant and easy to get on with. For the first time since his arrival at Compton Bobbin he found himself wishing that he had been there under slightly more creditable circumstances. It occurred to him that if Michael Lewes knew the truth he might easily regard him as quite an ordinary thief, since he was evidently a person rather lacking in humour. Lord Lewes broke in upon this train of thought by saying, after considering the matter for some moments, 'I think, you know, that the Egyptians themselves were more human than the Greeks, who always appear to have been so coldly perfect, like their own statuary, that it is difficult to credit them with the flesh and blood of ordinary human beings. "Fair Greece, sad relic of departed worth,"' he added mournfully, '"Immortal though no more, though fallen, great."'

Paul looked at him in some amazement. He had never, since his Oxford days, met anybody so fond of quoting.

'And presumably,' said Lord Lewes, 'that is how the Byzantinist must feel, otherwise I see no way to account for him. Attracted beyond words to the Archipelago itself, and repelled, I suppose, by the sheer perfection of the art which he finds there, he is obliged to search the islands for something which he thinks he can honestly admire. He ends, of course, by valuing the Byzantine quite absurdly high, far higher than its actual merit deserves.'

Paul, who was himself an ardent Byzantinist, and, like all such, extremely sensitive on the subject, was disgusted by this speech, which revealed in his opinion an intellectual dishonesty too dreadful to contemplate. He was just about to inform Lord Lewes that he was the author of a small and privately printed monograph entitled *The Byzantine Breakaway* when he remembered for the second time that evening that his position in the household was not of the most genuine, and that his name was now no longer Fotheringay but Fisher. Too angry to continue the discussion he walked quickly out of the room, saying over his shoulder to Philadelphia; 'I'll fetch that book I said I would lend you; I particularly want to know what you think about it.'

'Nice, isn't he?' said Michael as soon as he was out of the room.

'Awfully sweet,' said Bobby.

'He's an angel, I think,' said Philadelphia dreamily.

Later Lord Lewes said to his Aunt Gloria, 'What a really charming, cultured young man, that Mr. Fisher, it is a real pleasure to have made his acquaintance. I think you were so clever to find him. He is just the very person for Bobby, too; full of brains and yet most human.'

'Yes, he seems all right,' said Lady Bobbin. 'He was very much recommended to me. I only hope he will get the boy out of doors and make himself useful with Brenda Chadlington's brats. She announced to-day that she is bringing them again; most thoughtless and inconsiderate of her to my mind, but still—!'

Paul looked forward with no feelings of delight to his first ride to Compton Bobbin. He was, in fact, extremely terrified at the idea of it. Bobby, noticing his aversion to that form of exercise, tried to reassure him by pointing out that the distance to Mulberrie Farm was well under three miles, that it would be unnecessary for them to proceed at any pace more desperate than a walk, and that Boadicea, the mare which had been allotted to him to ride, was as quiet as any old cow; but in vain. Paul, most unfortunately for his own peace of mind, had happened to see the said mare out at exercise the day before, and had noticed in her a very different aspect from that of the ancient hireling on whose back he had spent so many painful hours jogging up and down the Rotten Row. To compare her to an old cow was simply silly. It was, in fact, only too apparent that here was a beast of pride and pedigree, who would almost certainly consider it a point of honour to cast the trembling tyro from her back. Paul knew, alas! how fatally easy, in his case, this would be; the smallest jerk, nay, even the transition between trot and canter, often proved sufficient to unseat him. He visualized with a shudder that horrid moment when everything would fly from his grip, the universe become black and roll several times round him, while the earth would suddenly rise up and bang him in the kidneys. It had happened in the soft and friendly Row and had been extraordinarily painful; what of the tarmac road, hard, black and shining like ebonite, which lay between Compton Bobbin and Mulberrie Farm? Poor Paul spent a wakeful night pondering these things, and by the morning had quite made up his mind that he would return to London sooner than court an end so sudden and unpleasing.

After breakfast, however, he felt more of a man again, and the sight of the precious red morocco volumes peeping from behind the schoolroom radiator put new courage into him. Besides, it would be a pity not to see a little more of Philadelphia. He was looking forward with some interest to hearing her verdict upon *Crazy Capers*, which he had lent her to read, saying that a friend of his had written it. Unsophisticated but intelligent, he thought, it was just possible that she might prove to be the one person who would put a proper construction on it. Possible, not likely. If she joined in the chorus of laughter he knew that he would be hurt, far more hurt than when Marcella had, who was always a hard, unimaginative little thing with a mind like a tennis ball. Meanwhile, fasting, for he felt too nervous to touch food at luncheon time, he prepared to face his ordeal.

By the most unlucky accident of fate Lady Bobbin happened to be talking to the stud groom in the stable yard when Paul and Bobby arrived there, and waited to see them mount. Paul, sadly conscious of the newness of his clothes, which had elicited roars of delight from the heartless Bobby as they left the house, stood a quaking and, no doubt, he thought bitterly, a pathetically comic figure, as he waited for Boadicea to be brought from her dark and smelly lair inside the stables.

'Cold, isn't it?' he said between chattering teeth to Lady Bobbin, who took no notice whatever of this remark. At that moment the snorting animal was led out, tossing her head from side to side in what seemed to be an ecstasy of rage and contempt, and showering little bits of froth in all directions. Paul, his unreasonable terror of horses now quite overcome by his unreasonable terror of Lady Bobbin, whose cold gimlet eye seemed to be reading his every emotion, decided that here was one of the few occasions in a man's life on which death would be preferable to dishonour, and advanced towards the mounting block with a slight swagger which he hoped was reminiscent of a French marquis approaching the scaffold. Grasping the reins and the pommel of the saddle firmly as he had been taught, he placed his left foot in the stirrup, when the animal, as indeed he had feared it probably would, began to wriggle its hind quarters away from him. When this had happened in the Row it had been his invariable custom to remove his foot from the stirrup and begin all over again. Now, however, feeling (he dared not look) that Lady Bobbin's eyes, not to mention the eyes of the stud groom, two under grooms, the stable boy, Bobby and two men who were carting away manure, were upon him, he rather lost his head and with the courage of despair gave a tremendous leap in pursuit of Boadicea's retreating back. To his immense astonishment, this piece of bravura was rewarded with complete success, and he found himself sitting fair and square in the saddle, with the stable boy placing his other foot in its appointed stirrup. Alas, he had not time to enjoy the fruits of triumph, as no sooner did the under groom, who was holding her, release Boadicea's head from his grasp than, despite Paul's frenzied tugs at the reins, she departed at a brisk trot out of the stable yard, and with a series of sickening slithers on to the tarmac road outside. Making a desperate effort, and by dint of counting out loud, one-two, one-two, Paul did manage to 'rise' in the approved Row style until he felt himself to be well out of Lady Bobbin's sight, when, abandoning all pride and self-respect, he clung with one hand to the saddle, jerked at the reins with the other and sobbed out in pitiful gasps: 'Stop, stop, dear Boadicea, whoa, whoa, Boadicea whoa, oh, please, please, stop!' The insensitive Boadicea, however, paid no attention to his pathetic cries, but continued to trot on, very nearly pulling him over from time to time by suddenly throwing her head right forward with loud and terrifying snorts. At last, when Paul felt himself to be at the end of his tether and, having long since abandoned both reins and stirrups, was looking out for a soft piece of grass on which he could hurl his aching bones, he heard another horse come up behind him. Bobby's outstretched hand seized the reins and, with a painful and alarming bump, Boadicea came to a standstill. She immediately began to eat grass at the side of the road, leaving, in the place where her head and neck had formerly been, a hideous gaping chasm. This was, for poor Paul, the last straw.

'I can't bear it, I can't bear it. I knew I should hate it. Lousy horse! Please, please let me get off and walk. Oh, what Gehenna!'

'It's all right,' said Bobby, who was laughing so much he could hardly speak. 'Oh, you did look too entrancing. I hope you'll do it again for me. No, no, don't get off, she'll walk quite quietly now as far as Amabelle's. Besides, you've got to get used to it, haven't you? But, you know, I can't think why she didn't come down, spanking along the tarmac like that. You should have taken her up on to the grass.'

'It's all very well for you to talk,' said Paul, who was still on the verge of tears; 'but I can't guide the beastly thing at all, it's as much as I can do to stay on its back.'

'My God, you looked funny,' said Bobby, rocking and guffawing. 'I'd give anything to see that again.'

Paul felt that, considering he had just been rescued from the jaws of death, he was not receiving that sympathy which was his due, and for some time he maintained a dignified silence. Presently, however, his sense of humour asserted itself, and he began to giggle too.

'I say, what will your mother have thought?' he asked rather nervously when he had recovered his breath.

'Well, by the mercy of Providence she was having a look at this horse's fetlocks when you got up, so I don't believe she noticed much. She did mutter something about "Why can't the blasted idiot wait a minute; what's all the damned hurry for?" But that doesn't mean a lot from her. No, you had a lucky escape this time, old boy. If you had let Boadicea down on the tarmac it would have been the end of Compton Bobbin and the journals for you, believe me.'

10

'One heart.'

'I double a heart.'

'Really, Sally, my sweet, don't you ride that convention to death just a little? It seems to be your one and only idea of a bid.'

'Well, I don't want to have to play the hand any more; I'd much rather you did, then there's no grumbling afterwards, you see.'

'I should have thought it would be more useful,' said Walter, ostentatiously looking at the score, 'at this stage in the proceedings, if you would show a suit.'

'Well, I've said before and I'll say again that I can't play bridge, and I don't like playing bridge. I only do it, as you know quite well, to make up a four. I think it's a horrible game, it makes everyone too bad-tempered and beastly for words—especially you, Walter darling, and you're apt to be quite nice at other times,' she added, for even when goaded to madness by Walter she always found it impossible to be unkind to him. 'Thank goodness Jerome comes to-morrow, and I shall be able to go back to my kiddies for Christmas like Mrs. Culbertson.'

'Darling, now don't be sour, please, my angel. I only meant that when you're playing you might try to concentrate a tiny bit more?'

'Concentrate! My head's aching with trying to concentrate, and all the thanks I get from you are these everlasting lectures, or else you sit there looking so reproachful and swallowing every time I play a card, as though I were doing it on purpose to annoy.'

'I said a heart,' murmured Bobby, who, having a superb hand, was anxious to get on with the business and had become rather restive during this family argument.

'Well, now, I've got to show a suit, have I?' said Sally.

'No, no! Of course not *now*,' cried Walter in that agony of impatience only known to the good bridge player obliged to suffer the vagaries of an absolutely incompetent partner. 'Not now, you can't. You've doubled a heart, haven't you? And you must stick at that. Paul says?'

'Two hearts,' said Paul.

'Two spades,' said Walter. 'Now, if Sally would only sometimes show a suit instead of sitting there saying double—'

'Oh, I'll show you the whole of my hand if you go on like this,' said Sally, 'and much good may it do you!'

'Four hearts,' said Bobby with an air of finality.

'Tee-hee,' he said as Paul put down a hand with six hearts to the ace, queen and an outside ace; 'now wasn't that just too psychic of me for words. Thanks ever so much, Paul, old boy—of course, you should have given me a double rise really, shouldn't you? But still—'

'What an extraordinary lead, Sally darling. Are you in your right senses?'

'Well, in that ghastly little book you made me read it said, "never lead from an ace, queen, never lead from a king, and never lead from a doubleton, it is a rotten lead". So that's the only thing for me to do, as far as I can see.'

'That's right,' said Bobby good-naturedly, 'tell him exactly what you've got in your hand; don't mind me, will you?'

Paul wandered over to the old world inglenook where Amabelle was sitting with Elspeth Paula on her knee.

'That's right, darling, have a good gurk,' she was saying, 'makes us all feel better, that does. Isn't she a treasure? Look at those huge goggling eyes. She's going to be a one with the chaps, she is. Aren't you, sweetikin. Boo!'

A confused murmur came from the bridge table.

'Now, Sally, out with it. There's only one lead you can possibly make.'

'I don't see that. I've got six cards in my hand and I can lead any of them, can't I? Oh, dear, I wish I knew.'

'Now, *think*. There's only one possible lead. Oh, my God,

you are a vile player, Sally. Well, now, that makes it all very O.K. for you, Bobby, game and rub—'

The butler opened the door and announced:

'Lord Lewes, madam.'

A perfectly stunned silence fell on Amabelle's drawing-room as Michael Lewes walked into it. Amabelle herself, who hardly ever showed emotion of any sort, turned crimson and nearly dropped the baby; Paul, feeling as he had not felt since, when at Eton, he was caught by the 'beaks' in the Slough cinema, made half a movement to escape through the garden door, but decided that this would only make matters far worse and that it would be better to stay and brazen it out; and the Monteaths gave each other long glances, fraught with meaning, over their cards. Bobby alone remained unshaken and went on playing the hand in his usual brisk and businesslike style. Such was the emotion of his adversaries that he made as a result not only four hearts giving him game and rubber, but little slam as well, a fact which he was heard afterwards loudly to lament. ('You know, Paul, it was monstrous only putting me up one. After all, you had the hearts; you knew I was calling on outside cards, didn't you? I naturally imagined you had a bare rise and wanted me to go to game. It is too maddening.')

The silence was broken by a shattering gurk from Elspeth Paula.

'What *savoir faire*!' said Bobby under his breath. 'Anybody would think I was the father. No more diamonds, Sally? Yes, I thought you had—no, no, that's O.K. The rest are good on the table, aren't they? That's one hundred and twenty below, one hundred overtricks and five hundred for the rubber. Thirteen I make it.'

'How are you, Michael?' Amabelle was saying. 'Ring the bell, will you, Paul? How lovely to see you, my dear. I can't think why, but I imagined you were still abroad. You know Mr. Fotheringay, do you?'

'Mr. Fisher?' said Lord Lewes.

'What am I thinking of—Mr. Fisher I mean, of course. And Walter and Sally you know, don't you? And this is the

Monteath heiress, Miss Elspeth Paula, who was born at one of my cocktail parties.'

'Indeed she wasn't,' cried Sally indignantly.

'Well, more nearly than I care to think about; if that taxi hadn't come when it did—'

'My dear, she wasn't born till four in the morning.'

'What a cheesey time,' said Bobby. 'Well, darling, we've finished our tiny rubber and I think we'd better be going. See you all to-morrow and thanks so much for having us. Come on, Paul, to horse, to horse!'

'Where are you off to, Sally?'

'I think I'd better take baby up to her beddie-bye. Come along then, you sweet precious.'

'I'm going to see Paul on his horse,' said Walter, chuckling, 'It sounds too good to be missed.'

Amabelle sighed. There was evidently a conspiracy to leave her alone with Lord Lewes.

'You look very well, my dear,' she said briskly, as the door shut on Walter and Sally. 'Did you enjoy yourself in Cairo?'

'No.'

'Oh, I'm sorry. I thought it all sounded so nice and interesting. I saw photos, in *The Sphere*, wasn't it? of a camp stool four thousand years old (or was it four hundred? I'm so bad at figures). Anyway, a very interesting old camp stool that you had found, and I thought how pleased you would be to find a lovely old camp stool like that,' said Amabelle desperately, making up the fire until it was a sort of burning fiery furnace.

'I shall never enjoy anything, and I shall never have a single moment's happiness in life until I can persuade you to marry me, Amabelle.'

'Oh dear. I hoped so much—I mean, surely Cairo must be full of lovely girls, isn't it? One's always reading about them, anyway. Haven't you changed your mind at all?'

'How could you imagine such a thing? No, indeed, I thought of you every moment of the day. I dreamt of you every moment of the night. I saw no beautiful girls, or if I did they looked to me like dolls stuffed with sawdust. Occasionally I came across people who knew you, they would mention your name in passing and it would go through me like a red-hot sword; if I saw in some illustrated paper a photograph of you it would make me even more wretched than I was already, and for days. Anything of beauty or of interest became intolerable because you were not there to share it with me. I tell you, you have made life very sad for me, Amabelle.'

'Dear Michael,' said Amabelle, stifling a yawn.

Curious, she thought, how some people have this devastating effect of boredom upon one. She had forgotten in three years just how much he did bore her, but the moment he had opened his mouth it had all come back to her in a wave and she was hopelessly, crushingly bored again.

'I'm so sorry, my dear,' she said.

'But I haven't come here to reproach you with that. I am here because I know, I feel quite certain that in your heart, only you won't admit it, you love me too.'

Amabelle was startled by this remark. Had she really behaved so badly as to lead him to suppose that this was the case? Or was it just his own vanity? 'Perhaps you think that because you wish it so much,' she said kindly.

'It's true, it must be true, I know it is. Only you are such an angel that you won't marry me because you think, quite mistakenly, that it would spoil my life, because you are older than I am and because of—'

'My international reputation?' Amabelle was of an age to think of reputation in these terms; in her young days a woman either had a good reputation or an international reputation, and, modern as she was in many ways, she never could quite rid her mind of these nineteenth century *nuances*.

'Yes,' she went on, 'I admit that is partly the reason. If I didn't feel certain that you would soon be very unhappy indeed I suppose I might make the sacrifice of marrying you. But in a short time you would be miserable, your career would be ruined for one thing' (international reputations and ruined careers went hand-in-hand when Amabelle was young), 'and besides that it is important for you to have children, and I'm not Sarah, you know, though in many ways a remarkable woman. But don't you see, Michael dear, that if I *were* in love with you I shouldn't consider any of that for five minutes. I'm far too selfish. I'm not in love with you. I like you I'm fond of you, and we have much in common. All that leads you to suppose that I'm in love with you, so now I must try and make you understand once and for all that I'm *not*. I'm *not*. And in any case I'm sick and tired to death of love. You must remember that for years it was my trade, my shop, my profession. Now I've retired, left my practice or whatever you like to call it, and I won't begin all over again. It bores me. I'm not strong enough to face the wear and tear and racket of a new love affair, with all the business of being your wife into the bargain; your relations who would come and see me, rightly as I think, to dissuade me from such a step, the sneers of the newspapers and of my own friends. Why should I be obliged to put up with all these things for something I don't even want? Because you must see, Michael, that, apart from any other consideration, if I marry you I lose instead of gaining a position. I become neither fish, flesh nor good red herring. In the case of James Fortescue it was quite different; he was an old man of the world when he married me and it was a good bargain for us both. He needed someone to keep his house, amuse his friends and be good company for himself; I needed a home and a name. We were both admirably suited, the best of friends, and, I think, very happy. I certainly was. This case is utterly different; if I married you we should each in our different ways lose much of what makes life bearable, but I honestly believe that I should lose more than you would. Anyhow, Michael, I am telling the truth, I swear to you that I am, when I say that nothing would influence me, none of these worldly considerations would prevent me from marrying you to-morrow if I loved you; but I don't love you. I don't, I don't, I don't. Is it possible that perhaps now at last you understand me?'

After making this speech Amabelle fell back on the sofa with a look of utter exhaustion and there was a long silence between them.

'Then what is to become of me?' said Michael bitterly.

'Oh, my dear, really I don't know. What does become of people who have been crossed in love? I never have been myself so I can't say from experience, but I imagine that sooner or later they meet somebody else who attracts them, mentally or physically, *et voilà! L'affaire est morte, vive l'affaire.* In your case let's hope it will be some nice, pretty girl who will make you very, very happy.'

'If you speak like that,' said Michael, 'it only shows that you can't understand the meaning of true love. Some people are made so that they can only love once in their lives.'

'Nobody is,' said Amabelle firmly. 'Unless, of course, they live with the person they love all their lives. Permanent and exclusive affection between married people may be possible but nobody can remain faithful to a person they never see. As for true love, I didn't believe in that until I met Walter and Sally, but I am really beginning to be very much afraid that in their case it does exist. Maddening, because it upsets all my theories about life.'

'You promise, then, that you don't love me at all, and that no argument, no persuasion will ever induce you to marry me?'

'No, Michael, I don't love you. I never have loved you and I never shall love you, and nothing that you can say or do will ever make me marry you. And I beg you, from the bottom of my heart, if we are to remain friends, that you won't bring up this subject any more.'

'Very well. I won't speak of it again. No woman has ever been so much loved as I have loved you, none has ever been so cherished and considered as I would have cherished and considered you if you had married me. Let that pass. I promise that I will never mention this subject to you again as long as I live, if you will promise that we can go on being friends?'

'Yes, of course, Michael dear,' said Amabelle gloomily. It seemed hard that she should have been at such pains to retire from Lewes Park on purpose to avoid this very boring scene, only to find that Michael was staying in the next house to hers.

'Are you staying at Compton Bobbin?'

'I arrived yesterday.'

'How did you find out that I was here?'

'By a fortunate chance. I happened to go for a little stroll before lunch with Bobby, and just as we got on to the Stow Road a large blue Bentley drove past, and Bobby said, "Oh, look, there's Amabelle's car." Not my usual luck, it would have been more like me to have stayed here three weeks without knowing that you were in the neighbourhood at all.'

Amabelle looked pensively into the fire. She did not and never had possessed a large blue Bentley. She thought out a few pungent observations which might be made to Sir Roderick when he came for his next game of bridge.

'Bobby is a very naughty little boy; he needs a thoroughly good spanking,' she said.

'It's really amazing how much he has grown up since I was in England last,' said Michael. 'Of course, it is three years, but even so it seems like a conjuring trick. When I left he was a little boy, rather young for his age. Now he is more like a man of thirty.'

'Eton does that for them. Bobby has a peculiar character, I must say. I suppose he is the one complete egotist of this generation. It is very lucky for him, because it means that he will never, in his whole life, know the meaning of the word boredom. He will always be quite happy so long as he is with other people, because it is wildly interesting to him to watch the effect that he is producing, and their reactions to his personality. If they like him, so much the better; if not, there is the entrancing problem of how to make them. Leave him alone and he would collapse, of course; but in company, of whatever description, he is contented and amused, and always will be. Perfect from his point of view, because he will never have to be alone in his whole life presumably, and for the rare occasions when loneliness will be forced upon him he has a certain weapon of self-defence, an absolutely inexhaustible facility for sleeping.'

'Yes, I should think that sums up his character pretty well,' said Michael, who had taken no great fancy for his cousin.

'And now that we are on the subject of Bobby, what's all this mystery about his tutor? Is he Fisher or is he Fotheringay?'

'By the way, yes, I must explain that to you, because it's all my doing really. His name is Paul Fotheringay, a great friend of mine. He very much wanted to read the journal of Lady Maria Bobbin with a view to writing her life. Your aunt wouldn't hear of lending it to him, which he very politely asked if she would do, so Bobby and I between us arranged for him to come down here under another name, as Bobby's tutor. You won't go and muck it all up, now will you, Michael darling?'

'Really, Amabelle, you are a baby. If you can play a trick on anybody you will. Poor Aunt Gloria; what a shame!'

'Honestly, I can't see any harm in it. In so far as anybody can have an influence over Bobby, Paul's will only be for the good, and as for the book on Lady Maria's Life and Works, I think it may be very well done and most amusing.'

'It will certainly be amusing, from what I remember of the journal,' said Michael, 'although it will probably be a case of laughing at and not with my poor great-grandmother. Philadelphia has become extraordinarily pretty since I saw her last, by the way.'

'Paul says she is so intelligent. He says she hardly ever speaks but that she has the most "heavenly instincts". I think he is falling in love with her, you know.'

Michael looked rather thoughtful on hearing this, and presently took his departure, saying, 'Good-bye then, my dear, dear friend. Please allow me to come and see you again soon. "Friendship," Lord Byron said, "is love without its wings," and that is a very consoling thought for me.'

When he had gone Amabelle went up to the nursery, where Elspeth Paula was having her evening meal.

'Oh, you cad,' she said to Sally, 'how could you have left me like that? You must have seen I didn't want to be alone with him; you are a monster, Sally darling.'

'It had to be, sooner or later,' said Sally calmly. 'Well what happened?'

'Oh, it was all most exhausting, you know, and frightfully

dull. The same old arguments over and over again, just like a debate on protection *versus* free trade, each side knowing exactly what the other will say next and neither having any intention whatever of being convinced. Poor Michael, it is quite funny really when you think that probably I would have married him if he'd been at all clever about it. But instead of putting it to me as a sensible business proposition he would drag in all this talk about love the whole time, and I simply can't bear those showerings of sentimentality. Otherwise I should most likely have married him ages ago.'

'Even boring as he is?'

'Yes, I think so. One never can tell, of course. It was all this nonsense about love that put me off so much. And of course he is a cracking old bore, isn't he?'

'When I was a girl,' said Sally, 'and before I met Walter, you know, I fixed a definite price at which I was willing to overlook boringness. As far as I can remember it was twenty-five thousand pounds a year. However, nothing more than twelve seemed to offer, so I married Walter instead.'

'You have always had such a sensible outlook,' said Amabelle approvingly. 'If I had a girl I should say to her, "Marry for love if you can, it won't last, but it is a very interesting experience and makes a good beginning in life. Later on, when you marry for money, for heaven's sake let it be big money. There are no other possible reasons for marrying at all."'

Michael Lewes walked back through the moonlight to Compton Bobbin in a most curious frame of mind. During his three years' absence abroad he had persuaded himself that Amabelle really and in her heart of hearts wanted to marry him; at the same time he was convinced that if (too terrible a thought to contemplate) by any unhappy chance he should prove to be wrong and if she should definitely refuse him, in such a manner as to make him feel certain that there was no hope of her ever changing her mind, under those circumstances he would be so very unhappy that he would undoubtedly feel tempted to commit suicide. He had sincerely thought that for him the prospect of life without her would be more than he would be able to bear. And yet now, strangely enough, he felt almost as though a load had been lifted from his shoulders, happier and more light-hearted than for months.

The truth was that during those three years he had made an imaginary picture of Amabelle in his own mind which had become, the longer he was away from home, the more unlike the real woman; until, on finding himself sitting with her, holding that first interview on which he had built so many hopes, he found himself sitting beside a stranger, and the image of Amabelle in his mind was shattered for ever. The things which he said to her then had little real meaning or conviction behind them. They were speeches which he had been rehearsing to himself for three years, and out of a sort of habit, a sort of loyalty to that self which had invented them, he repeated them to her. It was with no particular feeling, except perhaps that of relief, that he received in reply a final and definite refusal. And now, it seemed that the course of his life was delightfully plain before him. Having left diplomacy, a profession of which he was heartily tired, he would settle down at Lewes Park, take his seat in the House of Lords, and marry some pretty, well-born and delightful girl, someone, in fact, not unlike his cousin, Philadelphia Bobbin. He hummed a little tune as he walked.

11

Lady Bobbin was always most particular that the feast of Christmas should be kept by herself, her family and dependents at Compton Bobbin in what she was pleased to call 'good old-fashioned style'. In her mind, always rather a muddled organ, this entailed a fusion of the Christmas customs brought to his adopted country by the late Prince Consort with those which have been invented by the modern Roman Catholic school of Sussex Humorists in a desperate attempt to revive what they suppose to have been the merrieness of England as it was before she came to be ruled by sour Protestants. And this was odd, because Germans and Roman Catholics were ordinarily regarded by Lady Bobbin with wild abhorrence. Nothing, however, could deter her from being an ardent and convinced Merrie Englander. The maypole on the village green, or more usually, on account of pouring rain, in the village hall; nocturnal expeditions to the local Druid stones to see the sun rise over the Altar Stone, a feat which it was seldom obliging enough to perform; masques in the summer, madrigals in the winter and Morris dances all the year round were organized and led by Lady Bobbin with an energy which might well have been devoted to some better cause. This can be accounted for by the fact of her having a sort of idea that in Merrie England there had been much hunting, no motor cars and that her bugbear, socialism, was as yet unknown. All of which lent that imaginary period every attribute, in her eyes, of perfection.

But although each season of the year had its own merrie little rite it was at Christmas time that Lady Bobbin and her disciples in the neighbourhood really came into their own, the activities which she promoted during the rest of the year merely paving the way for an orgy of merrieness at Yule. Her first step in this direction was annually to summon at least thirty of the vast clan of Bobbin relations to spend the feast beneath their ancestral roof, and of these nearly twenty would, as a rule, find it convenient to obey. The remainder, even if their absence in Araby or Fair Kashmir rendered it palpably unlikely that they should accept, were always sent their invitation just the same. This was called Decent Family Feeling. Having gathered together all those of her late husband's relations who were available to come (her own had mostly died young from the rigours of tea planting in the Torrid Zone) she would then proceed to arrange for them to have a jolly Christmas. In this she was greatly helped by her brother-in-law, Lord Leamington Spa, who was also a fervent Merrie Englander, although, poor man, having been banished by poverty from his country estates and obliged to live all the year round in Eaton Square, he had but little scope for his activities in this direction. Those who should have been Lady Bobbin's prop and mainstay at such a time, her own children, regarded the whole thing with a sort of mirthful disgust very injurious to her feelings. Nothing, however, could deter her from her purpose, and every year at Compton Bobbin the German and the Sussex customs were made to play their appointed parts. Thus the Christmas Tree, Christmas stockings and other activities of Santa Claus, and the exchange through the post of endless cards and calendars (German); the mistletoe and holly decorations, the turkeys, the boar's head, and a succession of carol singers and mummers (Sussex Roman Catholic); and the unlimited opportunity to over-eat on every sort of unwholesome food washed down with honest beer, which forms the groundwork for both schools of thought, combined to provide the ingredients of Lady Bobbin's Christmas Pudding.

On Christmas Eve, therefore, various members of the vast Bobbin family began to arrive from every corner of the British Isles. The seven sisters of the late Sir Hudson, who, be it remembered, had all married well, of course brought with them their husbands and children, and in many cases their

dogs. It was noticeable that those who had married the least
well came first, by train, while, as the day wore on, richer and
ever richer motor cars, bedecked with larger and ever larger
coronets, made stately progress down the drive; until the St.
Neots Rolls-Royce made its strawberry-leaved appearance,
marking the end of this procession, just before dinner time.

Bobby, who for some while had been hovering round the
front door, greeted this vehicle with bloodcurdling screams of
delight, and rushed forward to assist from it his favourite
aunt, the Duchess of St. Neots and her daughter, his favourite
cousin, Miss Héloïse Potts. (The duchess had been married
five times, and had now settled down once more with her
girlhood's husband, the Duke of St. Neots, Miss Potts being
the offspring of an intermediate venture with an American
millionaire.)

To Paul the day was like an endless nightmare. Wherever
he went he met some new, and for the most part, unsympa-
thetic face, upon which the mutual embarrassment would
become intense. Lady Bobbin, unversed in social graces,
forbore to make any introductions, and Bobby spent most of
the day sulking in his bedroom. His mother had instructed
him to stay at home to greet his guests, the greater number of
whom, however, he was pleased to consider quite unworthy
of any notice.

Unluckily for himself, Paul happened to be the first down
to breakfast, when, entering the dining-room with a prodi-
gious yawn, he discovered six hungry Mackintoshes just off
the midnight express from Perth. They reminded him of
nothing so much as a Scotch family he had once seen on the
music halls, sandwiched between some performing seals and
a thin woman who gave imitations of (to him) unknown
actors and actresses. The children, a son of about seventeen
and three hideous girls of between ten and fourteen years old,
all wore tartan woollen stockings and long tartan kilts. Lady
Mackintosh was dressed in one, and Sir Alexander's reddish
whiskers fell into the porridge which he ate—Paul could
scarcely believe his eyes—standing up. Paul ventured a few
polite remarks, inquired about their journey and observed

that the weather was beautifully open, a cliché which he had learnt from Lady Bobbin, but as a family they appeared to be incapable of sustaining conversation, and he soon relapsed into that silence which they so evidently preferred. Presently Lady Bobbin came in from her early morning ride, and he was able to leave them to her hospitable ministrations.

Next to arrive were some more distant relations of Bobby's; Captain Chadlington, M.P., his wife Lady Brenda, their children Christopher Robin and Wendy, and a pack of ugly liver and white spaniels. They were being warmly congratulated by the rest of the party on Captain Chadlington's recent election to Parliament. Paul, having listened during lunch to some of his conversation, felt that it would be impossible to extend the congratulations to his electors; their choice of a representative seemed strangely unfortunate. He was evidently a young man of almost brutish stupidity, and Paul, who had hardly ever met any Conservative Members of Parliament before, was astounded to think that such a person could be tolerated for a moment at the seat of government. To hear him talking about Bolshevik Russia was a revelation to Paul, who took it for granted that Communism was now universally regarded as a high, though possibly a boring, ideal. Lady Bobbin's attitude towards it was just comprehensible, as she had evidently been out of touch with the world for years; but anybody who, being perforce in daily contact with persons of a certain intelligence, could still hold the views held by Captain Chadlington, must surely be a monster of denseness and stupidity.

Lord and Lady Leamington Spa came with their son, Squibby Almanack, whose appearance on the scene threw Paul into a fever of guilty terror since they had been at school together. He explained the situation to Bobby, who led his cousin into the schoolroom and told him the circumstances of Paul's presence in the house, upon which Squibby shook his fat sides, laughed a Wagnerian guffaw, and betook himself to the piano where he sat alone, picking out harmonious chords until it was time to dress for dinner.

Squibby Almanack was a person who belonged so

exclusively to one small circle of very intimate friends that any divorce, however temporary, from that circle left him in a most pitiable condition of aimlessness and boredom. In London he was never seen anywhere unless accompanied by 'Biggy' Lennox and 'Bunch' Tarradale, the three of them forming, so to speak, a kind of modern édition de luxe of *Les Trois Mousquetaires*. Of this fraternity that insouciant beguiler of womanhood, Maydew Morris, provided a picturesque if only occasional fourth, a sort of d'Artagnan, who, although of very different character to the others, was drawn to them by that passion for German music which was the dominant note in all their lives. In spite of the fact that Squibby, Biggy and Bunch sought no adventures save those of the questing spirit, while the adventures of Maydew were the talk of London, they being men of words while he was in all things a man of deeds; in spite of many dissimilarities of nature, the four of them got on well together, and there were very few classical concerts and no performances of German opera at which they could not be seen sitting side by side, deep in perusal of the score. They were further made remarkable by an extraordinary physical resemblance to each other. All four were on the large side, blond and with pink and white complexions, all, with the exception of the hirsute Maydew, slightly bald and quite lacking in eyebrows. They walked with the same peculiar gait, swinging rather prominent buttocks in the manner of hockey-playing schoolgirls, and all sat listening to music (which, provided, of course, that it came from the Fatherland, was the beginning and end of their existence) with the same air of rigid concentration.

Nearly always they sat alone, dispensing with female company. Sometimes, however, by mutual consent, each would appear followed by some pretty débutante; these, with gestures of exaggerated courtesy, would be motioned into the intervening seats, presented with programmes, and then be completely ignored. Many unlucky girls were forced to subdue their very natural distaste for highbrow music for hours on end in order that they might sit in this delicious proximity to their heroes, listening with awe to the Olympian breathing and even, if lucky, occasionally brushing a heroic hand. In the case of Maydew things sometimes went further during the dark moments of The Ring, but the other three were most consistently platonic in their friendships, and were rapidly becoming the despair of match-making mammas. Things were indeed beginning to reach such a pitch that the more ambitious mothers of sub-débutantes were obliged to abandon Paris as an educational centre and dispatch their daughters instead to Munich, where they could be trained to endure classical music silently and, in certain cases, even intelligently. For Squibby, Biggy, Bunch and Maydew were all highly eligible young men. After one of these 'mixed' evenings each would sternly criticize the girls produced by the others. Should one of them have yawned, or even sighed a little, her immediate expulsion from her admirer's visiting list would be demanded, while too frequent crossing and uncrossing of legs would be made a cause for bitter complaint. Poor Bunch, always less fortunate in his choice than the others, because more easily beguiled by a pretty face, produced two inveterate leg crossers on consecutive nights during the Wagner season and was very severely spoken to by Biggy, who, seated on the other side of these ladies, had suffered in consequence sundry kicks and knocks, and complained that his attention had been quite abstracted from the stage during several moving moments. It is true that the climax of horror was reached by a girl friend of Maydew who, during the Rhinegold, was heard to ask in a piercing whisper what the heaps of firewood were for, what the story was all about anyway, and whether there wouldn't soon be an interval; but then a certain licence was always allowed to Maydew in matters of the heart.

When the performance was concluded the girls, if any, were obliged to stifle their cravings for food, drinks and the gay sights of the town, and were hurried away in one or two unromantically full taxis to their respective homes. (Maydew's girl, however, always lived in a different part of London from the others and had to be taken home alone.)

After this, Squibby, Biggy and Bunch would foregather in

Biggy's flat, where they drank strong beer and talked of music and philosophy, and where, much later if at all, they might be joined by a complacent Maydew.

These friends were so seldom separated that Christmas time, when from a sense of duty Squibby, Biggy and Bunch would rejoin their noble families, seemed to them the most inhuman of feasts. How, secretly, did they envy the unregenerate Maydew, who had departed with a Balham beauty to Berlin in order to improve his German. Squibby in particular, dreaded all the year round the Christmas house party at Compton Bobbin. This year, however, things might be more amusing; he had been fond of Paul at Eton, Bobby was now a grownup person instead of a child, Michael Lewes, too, might prove to be pleasantly reformed. With less than his usual depression, he picked out some obscure motif from Siegfried.

The presence at Compton Bobbin of these people and others too numerous and boring to mention had the effect for the time being of throwing Philadelphia, Paul and Michael very much into each other's company. All three of them had a profound distaste for noise, crowds and organized pleasure, and they now spent most of their time hiding from the rest of the party. They went for long rides together every morning, Paul mounted, at his own urgent request, on an ancient cob which had long ago been turned out to enjoy a peaceful old age in the orchard, and which he found more to his liking than the aristocratic Boadicea. After dinner they would retire by mutual consent to the schoolroom and thus avoid the games of sardines, kick-the-bucket, and murders with which the others whiled away their evenings.

Bobby was now seldom to be seen; he spent most of his time giggling in corners with Miss Héloïse Potts, a pretty black-eyed little creature of seventeen who substituted parrot-like shrieks and screams of laughter for the more usual amenities of conversation, with apparently, since she was always surrounded by crowds of admiring young men, the greatest possible success. Even Squibby would often leave his beloved piano in order to enjoy her company, while at meal times her end of the table was eagerly sought after by all the men of the party, young and old, except for Paul and Michael. They, understanding neither her attraction nor her language (when she spoke at all she usually inserted the sound 'egi' after the consonants of her words, thus rendering her meaning far from clear to those unversed in this practice) would make their way with unhurried footsteps to the vacant places near Philadelphia. Indeed, everywhere else the conversation was too highly specialized to be very enjoyable. Héloïse, Bobby and their followers ended every sentence with 'egat thegi Regitz', which meant to the initiated 'at the Ritz'; Captain and Lady Brenda Chadlington, whose recent election to Parliament, actual and vicarious, had rather mounted to their heads, could speak of nothing but the P.M., S.B., L.G., the F.O., the L.C.C., the I.L.P., and their fellow M.P.s; the Mackintoshes fell upon their food in a famished silence, relieved, but very rarely, by remarks on the grouse disease; Lady Bobbin spoke to those about her of horses, hounds, and such obscure eventualities as going to ground, eating bedding, pecking while taking off, and being thoroughly well wormed; while Squibby, although quite intelligent, was apt to be a little wearisome with his musical talk or else a little exasperating with his theories on conditioned reflexes and other philosophical data.

Only Philadelphia, having no interests, talked no shop, but merely sat looking beautiful, calm and amiable, while Paul and Michael exchanged across her their cultured confidences, referring politely every now and then to her judgment. They both considered that although totally uneducated she was very far from being stupid, while the fact that what few books she had ever read had been written before the present century began gave to her mind and outlook a peculiar old-fashioned quality which Paul, at least, after the specious and metallic up-to-dateness of Marcella, found extremely restful.

As for Michael, he was consciously and most conveniently falling in love with her. For a day or two after his meeting with Amabelle he had been saddened and depressed. This was chiefly a retrospective feeling of regret for the last three years, embittered on account of what proved to have been a mere dream, a figment of his own imagination. Nature abhors a vacuum, and Michael had so extremely romantic a character that it was impossible for him not to imagine himself in love with somebody. His thoughts, therefore, turned almost immediately to his cousin Philadelphia, who, young, lovely, unsophisticated and intelligent, was clearly the sort of wife that a man in his position ought to have.

'I could never feel for her as I did for Amabelle,' he thought, as, in common with many people, he liked to believe himself only capable of loving once. 'All the same, what a charming wife she will make, and how happy I shall be with her!'

Lady Bobbin, who, with a mother's eye, saw clearly what was taking place, thought so too, as did young Sir Roderick. He had long intended that his sister should follow the example of his aunts in making a creditable alliance, and was delighted with this state of affairs. Philadelphia herself was happy in her new friends. She had a great respect for culture, and felt it to be a privilege that she was included in so many of their fascinating conversations. Of the two, however, she undoubtedly preferred Paul; Michael seemed to be rather grown up and alarming.

12

Christmas Day itself was organized by Lady Bobbin with the thoroughness and attention to detail of a general leading his army into battle. Not one moment of its enjoyment was left to chance or to the ingenuity of her guests; these received on Christmas Eve their marching orders, orders which must be obeyed to the letter on pain of death. Even Lady Bobbin, however, superwoman though she might be, could not prevent the day from being marked by a good deal of crossness, much over-eating, and a series of startling incidents.

The battle opened, as it were, with the Christmas stockings. These, in thickest worsted, bought specially for the occasion, were handed to the guests just before bedtime on Christmas Eve, with instructions that they were to be hung up on their bedposts by means of huge safety pins, which were also distributed. Lady Bobbin and her confederate, Lord Leamington Spa, then allowed a certain time to elapse until, judging that Morpheus would have descended upon the household, they sallied forth together (he arrayed in a white wig, beard and eyebrows and red dressing-gown, she clasping a large basket full of suitable presents) upon a stealthy noctambulation, during the course of which every stocking was neatly filled. The objects thus distributed were exactly the same every year, a curious and wonderful assortment including a pocket handkerchief, Old Moore's Almanack, a balloon not as yet blown up, a mouth organ, a ball of string, a penknife, an instrument for taking stones out of horses' shoes, a book of jokes, a puzzle, and, deep down in the woolly toe of the stocking, whence it would emerge in a rather hairy condition, a chocolate baby. Alas! Most of Lady Bobbin's guests felt that they would willingly have forgone these delightful but inexpensive objects in return for the night's sleep of which they were thus deprived. Forewarned though they were, the shadowy and terrifying appearance of Lord Leamington Spa fumbling about the foot of their beds in the light of a flickering candle gave most of them such a fearful start that all thoughts of sleep were banished for many hours to come.

For the lucky ones who did manage to doze off a rude shock was presently in store. At about five o'clock in the morning Master Christopher Robin Chadlington made a tour of the bedrooms, and having awoken each occupant in turn with a blast of his mouth organ, announced in a voice fraught with tragedy that Auntie Gloria had forgotten to put a chocolate baby in his stocking. 'Please might I have a bit of yours?' This quaint ruse was only too successful, and Christopher Robin acquired thereby no fewer than fourteen chocolate babies, all of which he ate before breakfast. The consequences, which were appalling, took place under the dining-room table at a moment when everybody else was busily opening the Christmas post. After this, weak but cheerful, young Master Chadlington spent the rest of the day in bed practising on his mouth organ.

By luncheon time any feelings of Christmas goodwill which the day and the religious service, duly attended by all, might have been expected to produce had quite evaporated, and towards the end of that meal the dining-room echoed with sounds of furious argument among the grown-ups. It was the duchess who began it. She said, in a clear, ringing voice which she knew must penetrate to the consciousness of Lady Bobbin:

'Yes, the day of the capitalist is over now, and a jolly good thing too.'

'May I ask,' said Lady Bobbin, rising like a trout to this remark and leaning across the projecting stomach of Lord Leamington Spa, 'why you, of all people, think that a good thing? Mind you, I don't admit that the capitalist system has come to an end, of course it hasn't, but why should you pretend to be pleased if it did? Affectation, I should call it.'

'No, not entirely affectation, Gloria darling. What I mean is that if, in a few years' time, people like us have no money left for luxuries we shall all, as a consequence, lead simpler and better lives. More fresh air, more sleep, more time to think and read. No night clubs, no Ritz, no Blue Train, less rushing about. And the result of that will be that we shall all be much happier. Don't you agree?'

Lady Bobbin, whose life was quite innocent of night clubs, the Ritz, and the Blue Train, and who had more time than she wanted in which to think and read, was not impressed by this statement. 'It has never been necessary to make a fool of oneself just because one happens to have money. There have always been plenty of decent people in the world, but unfortunately nobody ever hears about them, because they don't advertise themselves like the others. I wonder, Louisa, whether you will be quite so glad of the end of capitalism when you find yourself without the common necessities of life.'

'I don't anticipate that,' said the duchess comfortably. 'The world at present is suffering from over-production, not under-production, of the necessities of life.'

'Surely, duchess,' began Captain Chadlington ponderously, from his end of the table, feeling that now, if ever, was the time to make use of the information that he had so laboriously garnered from the P.M., the F.O., the I.L.P., S.B., L.G., and his fellow M.P.s, and to assert himself as a rising young politician. The duchess, however, took no notice of him and continued to goad Lady Bobbin.

'Think,' she said, 'how splendid it will be for our characters as a class if we are forced to lead simple, healthy lives, to look after our own children, and to earn our own bread. And then think of all the horrors that will be done away with, all those ghastly hideous country houses everywhere that will be pulled down. We shall be able to live in darling clean little cottages instead—'

'My house,' said Lady Bobbin, always quick to take offence, 'is, I hope, scrupulously kept. If you are implying—'

'Darling, don't be absurd. I only meant that they would be spiritually clean.'

'If you feel like this, Louisa,' said Lord Leamington Spa, now entering the lists with the light of battle in his eye, 'why on earth don't you act accordingly?' Why not shut up Brackenhampton and live in one of the cottages there instead? I don't suppose there's anything to prevent you.'

'Nothing to prevent me, indeed!' cried the duchess. She had been waiting for this argument to be produced like a cat waiting for a mouse. 'There are nearly a hundred living souls to prevent me, that's all. D'you realize that we employ altogether ninety-eight people in the house and gardens at Brackenhampton? I can't, for no reason at all, take a step which would deprive all those old friends of work, food, even of a shelter over their heads. It would be quite unthinkable. I only say that if the whole system by which we live at present were to be changed we ourselves would all be a good deal happier than we are, and better in every way.'

Lady Bobbin said 'Pooh!' and rose to leave the table. She was trembling with fury.

The afternoon was so wet and foggy, so extremely unseasonable, in fact, that Lady Bobbin was obliged with the utmost reluctance to abandon the paper chase which she had organized. Until four o'clock, therefore, the house party was left to enjoy in peace that exquisite discomfort which can only be produced by overfed slumberings in arm-chairs. At four punctually everybody assembled in the ballroom while for nearly an hour the Woodford school children mummed. It was the Woodford school children's annual burden to mum at Christmas; it was the annual burden of the inhabitants of Compton Bobbin to watch the mumming. Both sides, however, bore this infliction with fortitude, and no further awkwardness took place until after tea, when Lord Leamington Spa, having donned once more his dressing-gown and wig, was distributing gifts from the laden branches of the Christmas Tree. This was the big moment of the day. The tree, of course, immediately caught fire, but this was quite a usual occurrence, and the butler had no difficulty in putting it out. The real crisis occurred when Lady Bobbin opened the largish, square parcel which had 'To darling mummy from her very loving little Bobby' written on it, and which to Lady Bobbin's rage and horror was found to contain a volume entitled *The Sexual Life of Savages in Northern Melanesia*. This classic had been purchased at great expense by poor Bobby as a present for Paul; and had somehow changed places with *Tally Ho! Songs of Horse and Hound*, which was intended for his mother, and which, unluckily, was a volume of very similar size and shape. Bobby, never losing his head for an instant, explained volubly and in tones of utmost distress to his mother and the company in general that the shop must have sent the wrong book by mistake, and this explanation was rather ungraciously accepted. Greatly to Bobby's disgust, however, *The Sexual Life of Savages in Northern Melanesia* was presently consigned to the stoke-hole flames by Lady Bobbin in person.

The remaining time before dinner, which was early so that the children could come down, was spent by Bobby and Héloïse rushing about the house in a state of wild excitement. Paul suspected, and rightly as it turned out, that this excess of high spirits boded no good to somebody. It was quite obvious to the student of youthful psychology that some practical joke was on hand. He wondered rather nervously where the blow would fall.

It fell during dinner. Captain Chadlington was in the middle of telling Lady Bobbin what the P.M. had said to him about pig-breeding in the West of England when a loud whirring noise was heard under his chair. He looked down, rather startled, turned white to the lips at what he saw, sprang to his feet and said, in a voice of unnatural calm: 'Will the women and children please leave the room immediately. There is an infernal machine under my chair.' A moment of panic ensued. Bobby and Héloïse, almost too swift to apprehend his meaning, rushed to the door shrieking, 'A bomb, a bomb, we shall all be blown up,' while everyone else stood transfixed with horror, looking at the small black box under Captain Chadlington's chair as though uncertain of what they should do next. Paul alone remained perfectly calm. With great presence of mind he advanced towards the box, picked it up and conveyed it to the pantry sink, where he left it with the cold water tap running over it. This golden deed made him, jointly with Captain Chadlington, the hero of the hour. Lady Bobbin shook hands with him and said he was a very plucky young fellow and had saved all their lives, and he was overwhelmed with thanks and praise on every side. Captain Chadlington, too, was supposed to have shown wonderful fortitude in requesting the women and children to leave the room before mentioning his own danger. Only Bobby and Héloïse received no praise from anybody for their behaviour and were, indeed, more or less, sent to Coventry for the rest of the evening.

Captain Chadlington, secretly delighted to think that he was now of such importance politically that attempts were made on his life (he never doubted for a moment that this was the doing of Bolshevik agents) went off to telephone to the police. Bobby and Héloïse, listening round the corner, heard him say: 'Hullo, Woodford police? It is Captain Chadlington, M.P., speaking from Compton Bobbin. Look here, officer, there has just been an attempt to assassinate me. The Bolsheviks, I suppose. An infernal machine under my chair at dinner. Would you send somebody along to examine it at once, please, and inform Scotland Yard of what has happened?'

Lady Brenda said: 'I have always been afraid of something like this ever since Charlie made that speech against Bolshevism at Moreton-in-Marsh. Anyhow, we must be thankful that it was no worse.'

Lady Bobbin said that perhaps now the Government would do something about the Bolsheviks at last.

Lord Leamington Spa said that he didn't like it at all, which was quite true, he didn't, because on Christmas night after dinner he always sang 'The Mistletoe Bough' with great feeling and now it looked as though the others would be too busy talking about the bomb to listen to him.

Michael Lewes and Squibby Almanack dared to wonder whether it was really an infernal machine at all, but they only imparted this scepticism to each other.

The duchess said that of course it would be very good publicity for Charlie Chadlington, and she wondered—but added that perhaps, on the whole, he was too stupid to think of such a thing.

Captain Chadlington said that public men must expect this sort of thing and that he didn't mind for himself, but that it was just like those cowardly dagoes to attempt to blow up a parcel of women and children as well.

Everybody agreed that the tutor had behaved admirably.

'Where did you get it from?' Paul asked Bobby, whom he presently found giggling in the schoolroom with the inevitable Héloïse.

'A boy in my house made it for me last half; he says nobody will be able to tell that it's not a genuine bomb. In fact, it *is* a genuine one, practically, that's the beauty of it. Poor old Charlie Chad., he's most awfully pleased about the whole thing, isn't he, fussing about with those policemen like any old turkey cock. Oh! It all went off too, too beautifully, egI cegouldn't thegink egit fegunnegier, cegould yegou?'

'I think you're an odious child,' said Paul, 'and I've a very good mind to tell your mother about you.'

'That would rather take the gilt off your heroic action, though, wouldn't it, old boy?' said Bobby comfortably.

The local police, as Bobby's friend had truly predicted, were unable to make up their minds as to whether the machine was or was not an infernal one. Until this pretty point should be settled Captain Chadlington was allotted two human bulldogs who were instructed by Scotland Yard that they must guard his life with their own. A camp bed was immediately made up for one of these trusty fellows in the passage, across the captain's bedroom door, and the other was left to prowl about the house and garden all night, armed to the teeth.

'Darling,' said the Duchess to Bobby, as they went upstairs to bed after this exhausting day, 'have you seen the lovely man who's sleeping just outside my room? I don't know what your mother expects to happen, but one is only made of flesh and blood after all.'

'Well, for goodness sake, try to remember that you're a duchess again now,' said Bobby, kissing his aunt good night.

13

The two children of Captain and Lady Brenda Chadlington took a tremendous fancy to Paul, and he, although in the first place he had been completely put off by the fact that their names were Christopher Robin and Wendy, decided after a day or two that he would overlook this piece of affectation, which was, after all, not their own fault. He addressed them as George and Mabel (his lips refusing to utter their real names) and became very much attached to them.

'You see, it's not as though the poor things had chosen those names themselves,' he said to Bobby, 'and I should like to do what little I can to help them towards some form of self-respect. It is really tragic to see children surrounded by such an atmosphere of intellectual dishonesty. Poor George and Mabel.'

'What d'you mean?' asked Bobby, yawning. He was both bored and piqued, as Héloïse had gone off for the whole day with Squibby.

'In every respect,' went on Paul, 'they are treated as congenital half-wits by their parents. It is really shocking. They tell me,' he added disgustedly, 'that their Sussex house is called "The Cottage in the Wood". Well, I mean to say! I always refer to it as The Cedars when mentioning it to them. "The Cottage in the Wood" indeed; it's nearly as good as "Mulberrie Farm". I don't know what the English-speaking race is coming to.'

'Oh, of course, Brenda is the most affected woman in the world, we all know that, but she seems to be bringing them up quite nicely, I must say. They aren't at all spoilt or naughty.'

'They may not be. All I know is that their poor little minds are simply drowning in a welter of falsehood and pretence.'

'I s'pose you mean,' said Bobby, lighting a cigarette, 'that they are made to say their prayers and discouraged from seeing Brenda and Charlie naked in the bath. Personally, I'm rather old-fashioned about these things, too.'

'They are treated insanely. Not only are their brains being warped by constant application to the most sterile and insidiously unmoral forms of child literature—Barrie, A. A. Milne, Kenneth Grahame, Kipling, and so on—but they are being sternly repressed in every way. Just at this age when they should be opening out to life, assimilating new experiences of every sort, learning to care for truth and beauty in every form, they are subjected to constant humiliations, constant thwarting and hindering. Each little instinct has to be fought back as soon as it appears. How can they be expected to develop? Look at what happened to poor George on Christmas Day!'

'I didn't then and I should simply hate to now,' said Bobby, wondering when was the soonest that he could expect Héloïse back from her outing.

'Poor child, what could be more natural though? It was obviously the first time in his stunted little life that he had had the chance to eat as much chocolate as he really wanted. That incident told a tale of wanton cruelty.'

'Wanton greediness, I should call it. Dirty little pig.'

'As for Mabel, it is tragic to see the way she is chivvied about from pillar to post all day. "Have you washed your hands, Wendy? Did you clean your teeth? Take off your outdoor shoes. Get on with your knitting. Why haven't you brushed your hair? Put on your coat. Go for a walk." And all this, I would have you observe, to a child of inherently contemplative nature, a philosopher, probably, in the making. How *can* she develop properly? Every time she sits down to commune within herself, to think out some abstruse problem or to register some new experience, she is hounded off to perform dreary and perfunctory tasks. My heart bleeds for Mabel.'

'Wendy's the laziest little beast I know. She'd never do a thing if she were left to herself. It's pure idleness with her.'

'I entirely disagree with you, Bobby. That child has ideas and perceptions far beyond her age, and naturally they tire her out. She needs time and leisure in which to tabulate the impressions which she is always receiving from the outer world. Another thing very sad to see is the way her emotional life is threatened.'

'How d'you mean?'

'The poor child has a most distinct father-fixation, haven't you realized that? Very marked indeed.'

'Oh, nonsense, Paul; what extraordinary ideas you do have.'

'Nonsense, is it? My dear Bobby, just you notice the way she copies him in everything—she sits, walks, eats and talks exactly like him. Why, in another year or two she'll be the living image of him, always a sign of morbid affection, you know.'

'Really, you do surprise me. I suppose heredity could have nothing to do with it?' said Bobby sarcastically.

'Oh, no, nothing whatever. Nobody believes in hereditary influences nowadays. No, it's all the result of this mad passion she has, subconsciously, of course, for her father. Most dangerous.'

'Well,' said Bobby, 'I expect you know best. Anyhow, here comes one of the little cherubs, bless his tiny heart.'

'Mr. Fisher,' said Christopher Robin, putting his head round the schoolroom door. 'Please will you come out with us? Mother says we must go up the drive and back before lunch.'

'*Must, must,* always that word "*must*",' sighed Paul. 'So unwholesome, so stifling. Yes, I'd like to come out with you, George. Where's Mabel, then?'

'She's just looking for still-borns in *The Times*,' said Christopher Robin. 'I'll fetch her—oh, here she comes though.' Wendy Chadlington kept a little red pocket-book in which she wrote down the numbers of still-born babies every day as announced in the Births column of *The Times*. This lugubrious hobby seemed to afford her the deepest satisfaction.

'Any luck to-day?' asked Christopher Robin casually.

'Not to-day. One lot of triplets though. I keep a separate page for them, and there were two still-borns yesterday. One mustn't expect too much, you know.'

'Now George and Mabel,' said Paul, 'if you are quite ready let's go, shall we? There isn't much time, really, before lunch.'

Wendy looked at Christopher Robin and they both giggled. They were not, as yet, accustomed to their new names, and thought that Paul, though both amiable and entertaining, was undoubtedly a little mad.

Paul carefully replaced a volume of Lady Maria's journal behind the radiator, a practice that had but little meaning since Lady Bobbin, for whose deception it had been invented, never came near the schoolroom by any chance.

'What story are you going to tell us to-day?' asked Wendy as they started out.

'Please, Mr. Fisher, tell us a story about animals.'

'A true story about animals, please, Mr. Fisher.'

Yesterday's 'story', a homily on the life history of eels, had not really gone with much of a swing, and it was felt that a true story would be preferable to one which he had palpably invented himself.

'Well, let me think,' said Paul. 'I don't know many stories about animals. What kind of animal?'

'Any kind. *Please*, Mr. Fisher. You told us a lovely one yesterday,' said Christopher Robin encouragingly.

'I really *don't* know any,' said Paul, at his wits' end. 'Unless you'd like to hear one that I read in *Country Life* the other day. That was supposed to be true, I believe.'

'What's *Country Life*?'

'It's a paper your Aunt Gloria takes in.'

'*I* know,' said Wendy in tones of superiority, and added in a stage whisper: 'Christopher Robin can't read, you know, so of course papers aren't very interesting to him.'

'Pig,' said Christopher Robin. 'I *can* read. Anyway, *you*—'

Paul had been treated to arguments of this kind before, and hastily said: 'I'll tell you the story then, if you'll be quiet. A man was walking across a farm-yard—'

'A farmer?' asked Wendy, 'or a labourer?'

'If you interrupt I shan't go on. The man who wrote this story to *Country Life*—I don't know who he may have been—was walking across a farm-yard when he saw two rats running along in front of him. He threw a stick which he had in his hand at the first rat and killed it dead. To his great surprise the second rat, instead of running away, stood quite still as though it were waiting for something. The man thought this was so odd that he went over to look at it, and when he got quite near he saw that it was stone blind and had a straw in its mouth. The rat he had killed had been leading it along by the straw, you see, and the poor blind one thought it had stopped to have a drink or something, I suppose, and was just patiently waiting there for it to go on.'

'Well?' said Wendy after a pause.

'That's the end of the story.'

'But what did the man do with the blind rat?'

'I don't know. He didn't say in *Country Life*.'

'I should have kept it for a pet,' said Christopher Robin, 'and led it about on a straw.'

'I should *love* a dear little blind rat,' said Wendy, and added in a contemplative voice: 'I sometimes wish I were blind you know, so that I needn't see my tooth water after I've spat it.'

'I know what,' said Christopher Robin, 'let's pretend you're a blind rat, Wendy. Shut your eyes, you see, and put this straw in your mouth, and I'll put the other end of it in mine, and I'll lead you along by it.'

That evening Lady Brenda said to Paul: 'I think it is so kind of you to take my wee things out for walks (I'm afraid they *must* bore you rather, don't they?) but—please don't mind me saying this—don't you think that game you taught them with the straw is perhaps just the least little bit unhygienic? Of course if the straw could be sterilized I wouldn't mind, but you see one can't be certain where it came from, and I am so frightened always of T.B. So I've strictly forbidden them to play it any more, I hope you won't be angry; it's too sweet of you to bother with them,' and with a vague smile she drifted away.

*

Héloïse Potts took Squibby Almanack for a ride. She did this mainly in order to annoy Bobby, because she knew that she would be fearfully bored by Squibby before the day was over. They went, in the duchess's black Rolls-Royce, to visit Bunch Tarradale, whose ancestral home, Cracklesford Castle, was some thirty miles away, in Warwickshire.

Bunch was more than pleased to see them, and quickly led off Squibby to the downstairs lavatory so that they could have a good gossip.

'Have you heard from Biggy?' said Bunch, with more than a hint of malice in his voice. 'He's in love again.'

'Not again ! Who is it this time?'

'A girl called Susan Alveston. However, she's refused him, which is all to the good. Very ugly and stupid I hear she is, and only sixteen.'

'Biggy always likes them young though, doesn't he? How d'you know she's ugly and stupid?'

'He said so in his letter. He said "You might not call her strictly beautiful, but she has a most fascinating and expressive little face". That means she must be ugly, doesn't it, and all girls of sixteen are stupid. All the ones I've met are, anyhow. Besides, she must be, to refuse Biggy.'

'You seem to think that girls only have one idea in their heads, and that is to marry a lord as soon as they can.'

'Well, isn't that true?'

'*I* have my ideals,' said Squibby.

'And have you heard from Maydew?' continued Bunch. 'I had a picture post-card saying everything had turned out very satisfactorily.'

'So did I. Balham is evidently a success. What a sensible man Maydew is, to be sure, so untrammelled by feeling. It must be delightful to have a nature of that sort.' He sighed deeply. 'Anyhow, I am very glad about poor old Biggy, only I do feel that he should be more careful. One of these days he will be accepted, and how he would resent that.'

'So should we all. Do you think that perhaps my mother has now been subjected to the maddening prattle of your first cousin for long enough? Shall we relieve her?'

'Just a minute. I knew there was something else I wanted to ask you. What is all this nonsense about a quintet society?'

'Ah! Biggy has written to you about that, too, has he? Mind you, I think it's quite a good idea in some ways, only I'm afraid it's bound to be a failure if Biggy has anything to do with it. Still, I suppose one will have to join?'

'I suppose so. One must support the poor old boy, though, frankly, it seems rather a waste of his time and our money. It's so like Biggy, isn't it? Her always starts these wildly unpractical schemes. As though there were not enough good concerts as it is, besides, I hate listening to music in drawing-rooms. One's always catching people's eyes.'

'He tells me we shall be able to take off our boots.'

'I always do in any case.'

'All the same, I daresay there is something to be said for it, you know,' muttered Squibby grudgingly as they went upstairs. Fond as they were of each other, these friends had a sort of underlying bitterness in their characters which made it impossible for them not to indulge sometimes in a little harmless venom; like certain brothers and sisters, they always pretended to be sceptical of any venture embarked upon by others.

On the way home Miss Héloïse Potts took advantage of the darkness and the undoubted cold to snuggle very close to poor Squibby, who, overwhelmed by her proximity and by the kisses which soon fell upon his lips, responded in no uncertain manner and presently begged of her to marry him.

'No thanks, darling,' said Héloïse. 'I'm not old enough to marry yet. But when I am grown up I'm going to be either a duchess like mummy or a tart like Amabelle. Nothing in between for me. Only,' she added jauntily, 'there are rather few eligible dukes about so it almost looks as though—'

123

14

'DARLING EVELYN,

'*How* sweet, but oh, how *very* naughty of you to send me such
lovely links, at least I s'pose it was you who sent them, wasn't it?
Cartier very stupidly forgot to put in a card, but I don't know
anybody else who would be likely to do such a divine thing. I just
can't tell you how much I dote on them. I look at them all day and
think what an angel you are to give me a present like that, although
I do feel rather badly about not having sent *you* even a Christmas
card! However, I haven't forgotten the date of your birthday,
Evelyn dear. I have had a gorgeous Christmas. I do hope you have,
too. Amabelle, who has taken a house down here, gave me an
evening watch (platinum with diamonds round the edge) and
Auntie Loudie St. Neots a pair of gold hair-brushes, rather chi-chi,
but very attractive all the same, and I had altogether £60 in tips. But
far, far the best of all my presents do I like your exquisite links. See
you very soon, I hope. I may be in London for a few days towards
the end of the holidays, in which case we might lunch or something?
Anyway, mind you come trailing over to Eton some time next term,
won't you?

'Many more thanks for the lovely surprise.

'With love from

'BOBBY'.

Bobby folded up this letter, put it in an envelope, addressed it, and laid it in a pile of about six others, all couched
in exactly identical terms.

'Think of some more people for me to write to,' he said to
Paul, who was deeply engrossed in the journal.

'What sort of people?' asked Paul vaguely.

'The sort that might be taken in by a letter like this and
stump up something fairly reasonable.' He read Paul the
letter.

'That's rather a good idea, isn't it?' said Paul. 'I wish I was
brazen enough to do that sort of thing.'

'But I can't think of anybody else. You see, it must be someone rich, who enjoys giving presents. I won't risk taking all this trouble just to get a New Year's card back.'

'Nobody seems to enjoy giving me presents,' said Paul gloomily; 'and if they do their mothers go and burn the thing in the stoke-hole. It is hard—*The Sexual Life of Savages in Northern Melanesia* is a book I had always wanted most particularly too.'

'You can have *Tally Ho! Songs of Horse and Hound*, old boy. Here it is if you'd like it. I'm still wondering how they could have got mixed up. Do you think darling Héloïse might have had something to do with it?'

'I expect that's exactly what did happen. Thank heaven the little chatterbox isn't here any more. She gets on my nerves with her sudden shrieks and all that egi-egi.'

It was New Year's Day, and the entire house party had gone away that morning except for Lord Lewes, who remained alone and palely loitering, with the intention of very shortly laying his coronet, estates and person at the feet of his cousin, Philadelphia.

'She may be a little chatterbox,' said Bobby sourly, 'but nobody can deny that she is divinely attractive.'

'Indeed, *I* can.'

'And, as a matter of fact, I may quite likely marry her in years' and years' time,' went on Bobby, taking no notice of Paul. 'We are engaged now, if you want to know, secretly, of course.'

'My dear, she'll be married and have children before you're out of the cradle.'

'Oh, I don't expect to be her *first* husband, naturally. And you know, on second thoughts, I'm not at all sure I wouldn't rather marry Aunt Loudie. She's even more my cup of tea in many ways, and now it's allowed by law I shall consider it very seriously indeed.'

'Your mother told me most distinctly that aunts were not allowed. Only uncles, *she* said.'

'Oh, mother! She just makes up the rules as she goes along. I dare say she's guessed my guilty passion for Aunt Loudie and thinks she can throw cold water on it from the start. If one's allowed it's quite obvious that the other would be too. I wonder where Delphie is, by the way?'

'I think I saw her go out with Michael—for a walk, I suppose.'

'That's all to the good. Splendid. I'm very pleased about that.'

'Oh, you are, are you? May one ask why?'

'Well, naturally, I'm delighted when I see Delphie going about with Michael. I'm arranging for her to marry him, you know.'

'Oh, indeed! I thought he was supposed to be in love with Amabelle?'

'Love,' said Bobby pompously, 'has little or nothing to do with a matrimonial alliance. We Bobbins never marry, we contract alliances, and all that is necessary for a successful alliance is mutual respect. Now Michael's a sentimental old thing, and he likes to imagine that his heart is broken irreparably; it gives him a certain kick, I suppose. But that needn't prevent him from wanting to marry and settle down with a family of his own. Naturally he's not *in love* with Delphie, I don't see, personally, how one could be, but she would make him an ideal wife, healthy, well-born, properly educated for that sort of position, and so on. Just the very thing he ought to be looking for.'

'Oh, damn you,' said Paul.

'Now what's the matter?'

'Well, you see, I happen to be in love with her myself.'

'Oh, no! Are you honestly? How too enthralling this is. I wish I knew what you all see in her. But that's perfect. I hope Michael has noticed; it ought to egg him on no end, oughtn't it? A little rivalry and so forth. I must drop him a hint.'

'Do be serious for one minute, Bobby.'

'I *am*, dead serious.'

'You see, I want to marry her myself.'

'You want to marry her? Poor old boy, I'm afraid that's absolutely no cop. Delphie must marry well whatever happens. We Bobbins always do. Not that I wouldn't dote on

126

you for a brother-in-law if things were just a tiny bit different, but—you see?'

'You are a worldly little beast, Bobby,' said Paul gloomily, but without rancour.

'Yes, aren't I? It does pay so much better to be. I'm awfully sorry if you're feeling wretched about all this though, Paul dear, I am truly. I'm very fond of you, though you might not think it. Now I'll put these letters to be posted (let's hope they bring in a good fat return) and then we might ride over to Amabelle's, shall we? It's rather late, but we can always say that we stopped on the way back for a game of squash.'

At this moment Philadelphia wandered aimlessly into the room and asked what they were going to do.

'Where's Michael then?' said Bobby.

'I've no idea at all. Oh, yes, though, hasn't he gone out with mummy to look at that old barrow he's going to excavate?'

'Why didn't you want to go with them?'

'I thought it would be so boring.'

'Barrows,' said Bobby severely, 'are very far from boring, let me tell you. I think you should try to take more interest in such things. You seem to live in a walking swoon.'

'Anyway, what are you doing? Can't I come too?'

'We're only going to ride over for some squash in Woodford.'

'I'll come and watch.'

'All right, do,' said Bobby, in exasperation. 'Only I warn you there won't be much to watch. It's all a blind really, this squash and riding. We're really going over to see Amabelle Fortescue at Mulberrie Farm.'

'Oh, how thrilling. You know I heard mother talking to Auntie Loudie about her, and afterwards she forbade me ever to go near Mulberrie Farm.'

'Just you come along now then,' said Paul. 'Amabelle is longing to meet you, I know, and this is an excellent opportunity.'

On their way to the stables Bobby drew Paul aside and said: 'Now we must try and make her pay attention to that

127

barrow, community of interests is supposed to be an essential of married happiness.'

'Damn you,' said Paul again.

They found the party at Mulberrie Farm scattered about the drawing-room in attitudes of deathlike exhaustion.

'We're awfully tired and ill to-day, darlings,' said Amabelle, 'but it's always lovely to see you, and I'm glad you've brought your sister at last, Bobby dear.' She lay curled up on a Knole sofa and appeared almost unable to open her eyes. Her voice had become a mere whisper, her face a grey mask on which the rouge showed up with startling intensity. Her eyelashes, which she always painted navy blue, were now no darker than the shadows beneath them. Even the tactful Bobby was hardly able to conceal the shock that her appearance had given him. Sally and Jerome lay on other sofas, their ravaged faces half buried in pillows. Walter was nowhere to be seen.

'What on earth is the matter with you all?' said Bobby, after surveying this scene for some minutes in silence. 'I know, you've been having a blind,' he added accusingly.

Amabelle, who had dropped off to sleep again, woke with a start and said, 'That's it, however did you guess? We got to bed at half-past eight this morning, if you want to know, and we should be there still if it wasn't for Sally's perfectly idiotic theory that it makes one feel better to get up for tea. I can't say I've noticed it. I couldn't possibly feel more awful myself.'

'What on earth have you been doing that could keep you up until eight-thirty; and why didn't you invite me to the ball?'

'We went to the New Year party at the Albert Hall. Sally suggested it at dinner last night, so we just bundled ourselves into fancy dress and popped up to London in the car. Oh, how I wish we hadn't, too!'

'Oh, cads!' said Bobby, and his eyes quite literally filled with tears. It was always a very real sorrow to him if he missed a party of any kind. He felt cross and resentful.

Amabelle saw this at once; she knew her little Bobby. 'Darling, you can't imagine how much we all longed for you

128

to come,' she said quickly, 'but I simply couldn't think of taking you, for your own sake, my sweet. You must remember that it never pays to risk quarrelling with one's bread and butter, and you've got to keep in your mamma's good books, especially if you're not to be packed off to Sandhurst, eh? So don't look quite so sad, precious.'

'Oh, well, I see your point, I suppose. Actually, of course, it could have been worked quite safely; still, never mind, it's all over now. Was it lovely?'

'It was lovely,' said Sally, sitting up with an obvious effort, and powdering her nose. 'Simply grand. I got off with a miner from Lancashire, who had just absconded with the local slate club money and was having the time of his life in London on the proceeds. He was a great wit; he said the lady miners are minarets—he made that sort of joke. He was that sort of man, you see. Heavenly. And he said "I know where I've met you before, with Lady Alistair Grayson in her villa at Antibes," and I said "You can't have met me there because I don't know the old trout," and he said, "Oh, nor do I, of course. But I always read about her parties in the papers." That is the sort of man he was—very O.K. I had a great romance with him. And who Walter got off with no one knows because he vanished half-way through the party, you see, and hasn't come back yet. He must be having a gorgeous time.'

Sally rose uncertainly to her feet and staggered upstairs.

'Poor darling Sally,' said Amabelle. 'I must say she does behave well on these occasions. I admire her for it a good deal. It's really too naughty of Walter not to ring her up or something; he must know by now how much she always worries.'

'There's your groom,' said Bobby, who hated hearing about other people's troubles, and had wandered over to the window, 'galloping Paul's horse round and round that field; he is a divine man. Fielden, our groom, told mother that he'd never known me to take so much interest in riding, or exercise the horses so thoroughly before, as I do these hols.; and of course the old girl puts it down entirely to Paul's wonderful influence. Tell me some more about that party you so kindly asked me to.'

'It was just like any other party of that sort. It had every element of discomfort and boredom and yet for no particular reason that one could see, it was divine fun. It's not often one finds English people really gay, is it? And in the Albert Hall of all places, in that odour of Sunday afternoon concerts, it is quite astonishing.'

'Who was there?'

'Everybody in the world. The improper duchess for one.'

'With Héloïse?'

'I didn't see her, but she may have been too well disguised. Jane and Albert were there, just back from Paris.'

'Were they, now?' said Paul with interest. 'And how are they? Happy?'

'Wretched, I believe. Did they expect anything else? What a silly marriage that was, to be sure.'

'Oh dear,' said Paul glomily, 'it really is rather disillusioning. When one's friends marry for money they are wretched, when they marry for love it is worse. What is the proper thing to marry for, I should like to know?'

'The trouble is,' said Amabelle, looking at Philadelphia whom she thought surprisingly beautiful, 'that people seem to expect happiness in life. I can't imagine why; but they do. They are unhappy before they marry, and they imagine to themselves that the reason of their unhappiness will be removed when they are married. When it isn't they blame the other person, which is clearly absurd. I believe that is what generally starts the trouble.'

'I expect that's quite right,' said Paul, sighing.

'In any case,' Amabelle went on, 'the older I get the more I think it is fatal to marry for love. The mere fact of being in love with somebody is a very good reason for not marrying them, in my opinion. It brings much more unhappiness than anything else. Look at Sally. Every time Walter leaves the house for half an hour she thinks he will be run over by a bus and on an occasion like this it's impossible to guess what she must be suffering. Now, supposing she weren't in love with him, she'd be feeling ghastly now, like I am; but she wouldn't be frightfully unhappy as well, and on ordinary occasions she could enjoy her life peacefully. What does Bobby think about it?'

Bobby said, 'Just what I told you, see?' to Paul, and to Amabelle, 'I still think it's lousy of you not to have taken me last night. I shan't get over it for ages and ages. As for marriage, I fully intend to marry you, darling, when I'm a bit older and have had my fling, you know. We'll live where it's hot, shall we? and adopt four black children and be as happy as the day is long.'

'You are a fool, Bobby. I'm very glad you've brought your beautiful sister here at last,' said Amabelle. Philadelphia blushed, she was unused to being thought beautiful. 'She must come again soon, when we're not all so tired and sad. Where's Michael, by the way? Still at Compton Bobbin?'

'Oh, yes, rather,' said Bobby. 'He's gone out to look for a barrow to excavate, I believe.'

'Gosh! how boring.'

'No, no, not at all boring, you know, really. Barrow digging is a fascinating occupation.'

'Is that a car coming up the drive?' said Amabelle languidly. It was getting dark, and the sidelights of a car flashed into the room.

'Yes, it is. A huge Daimler, with Walter in it. Ha, ha, that's funny; the old boy's still in fancy dress.'

Waslter came in rather sheepishly, still wearing his *matelôt* clothes of the night before, and borrowed some money from Jerome to pay for the car, which was a Daimler hire. This done, he came back again, lit a cigarette and said in an exaggeratedly casual voice, 'Sally all right?'

'I suppose so; I don't imagine she's awake yet really. Did you have a good time?'

'No, lousy. Why on earth did you go away like that without me?' Walter flung himself out of the room.

'Hity-tity,' said Amabelle. 'So that's the tone, is it? Well, so long as one knows. How much did you lend him, Jerome darling?'

'A fiver,' said Jerome, who was now sitting up and reading *The Times*.

131

'I'll give it to you myself. It was rather a shame, I suppose, leaving him there. Still, half-past six, you know, and he hadn't been seen by anyone since midnight.'

'There are trains,' said Jerome, pursuing his own line of thought, 'and road coaches.'

'In those clothes? I hardly think he could have.'

'He had an overcoat. He must know he can't afford Daimler hires. It would have been more honest.'

'It would have been most unlike Walter. How goes the journal, Paul?'

'Grand. I'm reading the first volume now. This morning I got to where "Dearest Mamma very kindly gave me permission to go a little way into the shrubbery with Sir Josiah Bobbin, and while there he said that it would make him very happy if I should become his wife. I replied in some agitation, due to the beatings of my poor heart, that my future must be decided by dearest Mamma and dear Papa; whereupon he told me, to my immeasurable joy, that he had already solicited and obtained their consent to our union. We then went back into the drawing-room, where I was embraced by dearest Mamma, dear Papa and all my dear brothers and sisters, also by poor Aunt Agatha, who all said that they hoped I should be very very happy. It was a most touching scene, and I felt quite *faint* from joy and emotion." Isn't it exquisite?' said Paul enthusiastically. 'The account of her wedding is too perfect; I can't remember that exactly, but I'll bring it along sometime. You know, Amabelle, I think I shall be able to write something unusually good after this, thanks entirely to you and Bobby, of course.'

'Don't mention it, old boy,' said Bobby. 'Just remember me in your dedication, though. "To my friend, Sir Roderick Bobbin, Bt., great grandson of Lady Maria, without whose help, encouragement and never failing sympathy this book could hardly have been written." Something on those lines, you know.'

Paul said nothing. He intended to dedicate the 'Life' to Philadelphia Bobbin.

15

Shortly after the New Year, foot and mouth disease vanished
from the cow-sheds of Gloucestershire, and the Bobbin hunt
was able to resume its season. Lady Bobbin was now rarely to
be seen between breakfast, at which meal she would appear
booted and spurred to eat vast quantities of meaty foods, and
tea-time, when she would loudly re-live the day for the
benefit of Philadelphia, Paul and Michael. Her accounts of
what had happened were always interspersed with bitter
criticisms of the young female members of the hunt, who,
according to her description of their appearance, might be
supposed to come out hunting in full evening dress and with
the sole idea of abstracting the attention of their men friends
from the serious business on hand.

'There was Maisie Critchley, in a pink shirt and a satin
stock (I know you'll hardly believe me), made up to the eyes
and her hair all fuzzed out under her bowler. Perfectly
disgusting. I can't imagine why she bothers to get up on a
horse at all; she can't go for nuts and she spends her whole
time coffee-housing with young Walters. Then, of course, he's
too busy holding her horse while she makes up her face and so
on to think of anything else. I don't know what the young
people are coming to. Lucky thing my poor father is dead,
that's what I say. It would have broken his heart to see all
these goings-on.'

Paul, hoping to see some painted sirens, went to one or two
meets; but the women seemed to him, young and old, to be of
a uniform plainness, with hard, weather-beaten faces entirely
devoid of any artificial aids to beauty. He could only suppose
that Lady Bobbin, in the delirium of the chase, was subject to
hallucinations which took the form of satin stocks and pretty
painted faces.

Bobby, who, rather against his will, admitted to a fondness for hunting, usually accompanied his mother and stayed out most of the day; but Philadelphia, since having as a child broken nearly every bone in her body when her pony fell at a stone wall out cubbing, had no nerve left. She and Paul now spent their time between Mulberrie Farm, both Sally and Amabelle having taken a great fancy to her, and the barrow, where Michael was busily conducting excavations with the aid of four members of the local unemployed.

'That book you lent me,' she said one morning as they were walking towards the barrow; 'I finished it in bed last night. It's very sad, isn't it?'

Paul looked at her with positive rapture.

'Did you really think so?' he said incredulously.

'Yes, of course. It is dreadful—I cried at the end.'

'Oh, you *didn't*, Philadelphia?'

'Yes, I did. Why, don't you think it's very sad?'

'I do. But nobody else does, you know. They don't understand it; all the reviewers thought it was meant to be a funny book.'

'How could they? How perfectly absurd. I think it's too terrible, and wonderfully written, isn't it? Poor Leander Strutt, he was so happy at Oxford, d'you remember? And so miserable when he was working for the pawnbroker. I'm sure that must be true of certain young men. I'm sure lots of them are happy until they leave their university and then never happy any more.'

'Indeed,' said Paul eagerly, 'you are so right. I was just like that myself. I don't believe I shall ever be as happy again as I was at Oxford.'

'It is different for girls, of course. I had a dreadful childhood; I was wretched the whole time. How I longed to be grown-up!'

'And now that you are grown-up, is it any better?'

'Up to now I haven't thought so. I came out in London, you know, about three years ago, and went to parties, which I simply hated. I didn't like the people I met, and they didn't like me either. Since then I've just lived down here, with nothing to do and no friends, and been even more miserable than I was as a child. But I've always felt that there must be people somewhere in the world whom I could like and get on with, and I see that I was right.' She paused a moment, and then said, 'Now that you and Sally and Amabelle and Michael have all appeared in my life I'm very happy indeed. I don't know what I shall do when you all go away.' Her eyes filled with tears as she said this.

Paul felt rather annoyed at the inclusion of Michael's name in this group of superior beings.

'I've got a great secret to tell you,' he said.

'Have you? What?'

'*I* wrote *Crazy Capers*.'

'*You* did, Paul? Oh, how thrilling. I do feel excited to think that I know a real author at last. But how clever you must be; as clever as Michael I should think, or even cleverer. It is a lovely book. I don't understand, though, why you wrote under another name; I should want everyone to know that I was the author if I wrote something so wonderful.'

'My real name,' said Paul, '*is* Fotheringay. Fisher was my mother's name.' And he told her why he had come to Compton Bobbin. 'Thank God I did,' he added, looking at her lovely face.

After this conversation Paul appeared in a new light to Philadelphia. She had already felt that she might fall in love with him, now she knew that she had done so. An author in disguise is a more heroic figure than a holiday tutor.

They arrived at the barrow to find Michael in his shirt-sleeves, grouting about in the bottom of a hole, now about five feet deep, which had been dug by the workmen.

'We may strike the treasure at any moment now,' he cried, in a voice strangled with excitement. 'At any moment we may come upon the charred bones of the great Viking and his wives, the human ashes, surrounded by great spears and shields and gleaming gold ornaments, painted sherds and jewelled necklaces.'

Paul and Philadelphia, fired by his enthusiasm, leapt into the pit and began feverishly to dig.

'Be careful,' cried Michael, in great agitation. 'All this earth must be properly sifted. I think perhaps you had better leave it to me; you can stand on the edge there, if you like.'

This proved, however, in the bitter east wind that was blowing, to be rather a chilly occupation, and they very soon went home again.

That afternoon, coming in from a visit to Mulberrie Farm, they were met by Michael, who almost screamed, 'Come and see, come and see. I've found him; I've found the Viking with all his ornaments, great painted sherds, gold breastplates—'

'Where—where?'

'On the billiard table.'

They rushed to the billiard-room, where they found, reposing on newspaper, a small heap of earthy objects. There was a bit of bone, a square inch of what looked like broken flowerpot, some apparently meaningless pieces of metal and a tiny gold wire. These were the great skeleton, the sherds, the spears and shields, the jewelled necklaces for which Michael had so perseveringly and so expensively been searching. Such, however, is the power of an archaeological imagination that Michael himself, able to reconstruct out of these bits and pieces the objects of which they had (perhaps) originally formed a part, regarded them as a most valuable and interesting addition to modern knowledge. His gratification knew no bounds when, having dispatched his treasure to the British Museum, that revered institution graciously accepted it. (The piece of bone, however, under expert examination, proved to be not that of a Viking but of a pig.)

16

The point-to-point meeting of the South Cotswold hunt took place in some of Major Stanworth's fields. To celebrate the occasion, Amabelle gave a lunch party which consisted of the Monteaths, Major Stanworth, his little boy Adolphus and Paul. Bobby, who had, of course, been invited, was obliged, greatly to his disgust, to attend a farmers' luncheon in a large, damp and evil-smelling tent on the race-course itself. In the absence of his always cheerful rattle the party at Mulberrie Farm settled down to a meal of unrelieved gloom. Sally made no attempt to conceal her wretchedness and never for one moment stopped crying, her emotion being due to the fact that, in spite of all her efforts to prevent such a thing from happening, Major Stanworth had lent Walter one of his horses to ride in the nomination race. Nobody liked to break in upon her too evident grief with a merry remark, and her tears, though of the unobtrusive variety, stealing down her cheeks one by one instead of gushing forth in uncontrolled abandon, had a most depressing effect on the general spirits. Major Stanworth, a kindly and not insensitive soul, was perfectly well aware that poor Sally regarded him as a particularly low and evil type of murderer, and kept on making pathetic little advances to this unresponsive Niobe.

'Really, Mrs Monteath,' he said nervously, 'you need not feel in the least upset. I assure you, there is no need to worry like this. Old Foxtall, the horse that Walter is going to ride, has never put a foot wrong in his life, never. Please believe me. He may be a bit slow, but there's no safer ride in the country. Surely you must realize that I would never think of putting Walter up on one of my horses unless I knew that it was perfectly safe—would I, Mrs Fortescue?'

'No, of course not, darling,' said Amabelle, looking at him

137

affectionately; 'but all the same, I do think it's rather dreadful for my poor Sally, and none of us are blessing you exactly, because now, you see, we shall all have to go out in this ghastly east wind to see Walter doing or dying, whereas otherwise we might have drunk our cherry brandy by the fire and imagined ourselves at the point-to-point instead. Now, Walter dear, before I forget, I mean to bet five shillings on you, not that I imagine for a moment that I shall win anything, but just for old sake's sake, don't you know.'

'Each way, or win only?' said Walter professionally. ('If you don't stop crying like this, Sally, I shall divorce you—I wish you'd try to be more controlled on these occasions; think of the women of Sparta, can't you?) It may make all the difference to my tactics when approaching the last fence. You see, if it's win only I might feel obliged to bump and bore a bit, otherwise I should probably sit tight and get a comfortable third. So make up your mind and let me know, will you?'

'That's all right, old boy,' said Paul. 'You ride a really filthy race. Above all, don't miss any opportunity to cross Captain Chadlington; he's riding a horse called Stout Unionist (out of True Blue by Brewery) and I shall die if he wins.'

'Oh, so he's back again, is he?'

'Yes, he came back for the point-to-point last night.'

'How's the Infernal Machine?'

'Grand. He's going to ask a question about it in the House.'

'I think we should be going on out,' said Amabelle, 'although a more unpleasant idea in this weather I can hardly imagine, myself! Just listen to the wind, howling down the chimney—ugh! Come on, Sally, my poor darling, I can lend you a fur coat and a nice big hankie, and we might tie hotwater bottles next to our tummies, don't you think? Very nice and pregnant we shall look, too.' She led the weeping Sally from the room.

'You'll be blind, you know, Walter, old boy, if I may say so,' remarked Paul, who had been watching Walter fill his glass with unusual abandon.

'Yes, I mean to be,' said Walter. 'I'm terrified,' he added

confidentially as Major Stanworth left the room, 'never been so frightened in my life. But nothing hurts nearly so much if you're drunk, does it? I once saw a drunk man fall thirty feet, on to a stone pavement, too; he wasn't hurt a bit. Come on, then; are we all ready for the pretty spectacle of my demise? Cheer up, Sally, think of the Roman matrons, darling. Besides, you're quite attractive enough to get some more husbands, though, of course, I doubt you finding anything quite up to my form again. Have we got lots of cherry brandy in the car?'

The point-to-point course lay on the exposed and wind-swept side of a hill and the cold which assailed Amabelle's party on their arrival at this scene of action was beyond what would be thought possible by anyone not accustomed to the pleasures of rural England in winter. Walter, by now fairly drunk, got out of the car and strode about in his overcoat, accompanied by Major Stanworth, Paul and Bobby. He went down to look at the water jump, had a talk to Major Stanworth's groom, and generally behaved in what he imagined to be a professional manner. Amabelle and Sally huddled up together for warmth in the Rolls-Royce, clasping innumerable hot-water bottles, and refusing to move out of it until Walter's race should begin. This was third on the programme. After the first race, at which there were many accidents, poor Sally was even further depressed by seeing the motor ambulance leave the course with its groaning load. A reserve of pride in her nature, however, prevented her from making any more scenes, and it was with a comparatively cheerful face that she went off to the paddock when the time came for Walter to mount. Amabelle still declared that nothing would drag her from the car, so Paul took Sally under his protection. He pointed out Captain Chadlington, whose ordinarily red face was now mauve from cold and har-monized unpleasingly with his racing colours of black, cerise cap and old-gold sleeves. Lady Brenda, in expensive tweeds and holding a brown leather shooting stick, was talking to friends nearby; it seemed to Sally that she was viewing her husband's approaching peril with unnatural calm.

'You can go into the paddock, if you like, Sally,' said Bobby, who was accompanied by a pretty little Jewess with thin legs and a spotted scarf.

'Oh, I shouldn't dare,' shivered Sally, 'your mother looks too forbidding to-day, doesn't she? Besides, Lady Prague is in there.'

At last the terrible moment came and the crowd round the paddock drew back to make a path for the horses, who jogged off with much tossing of heads and jingling of harness towards the start. They were soon lost to sight over the brow of the hill, and Walter was last seen leading the field at an uncontrolled gallop and fishing madly in the air for a stirrup with his left foot.

'Now,' said Paul, taking Sally's arm in a fatherly manner, 'where would you like to go? Shall we watch the race from the winning post or would you rather be at one of the jumps?'

'Where is he most likely to be killed?' asked Sally, her teeth chattering. She was by now in a state of utter resignation, regarding herself as a widow already; she felt, however, that she would like to be at hand to close Walter's eyes and hear his dying words, if any.

'Sally, dear, please don't be so absurd. Walter rode in several grinds at Oxford. I remember it quite well,' lied Paul, 'and he never had a scratch. I promise faithfully that he'll be all right—do stop worrying. Let's go to the last jump of all, shall we? Giles Stanworth says we can see most of the course and the finish from there.'

'Just as you like,' said Sally in a dull voice. She was wondering vaguely which of her male acquaintances she could bear to marry in the event of Walter's death.

Presently there was a murmur all over the race course, somebody in the crowd said 'They're off,' and a distant thunder of hoofs could be heard.

'There,' said Paul triumphantly, 'what did I tell you? They're all over the first jump. Walter's among the first three; can you see? Would you like these glasses?'

140

'No thanks,' said Sally. 'I never can see anything but sky through them.'

'I believe Walter's bound to win, you know; all over the second jump and he's still leading. Isn't it grand. Cheer up, Sally, it'll soon be over. Now they go round the hill and we shan't see them for a minute or two.'

A voice in the crowd behind was heard to say confidentially: 'Here, photographer—I'm Sir Roderick Bobbin and that's my cousin, Lady Brenda Chadlington, in the beige hat. If you take our photographs you'll get promotion, I should think.' And a moment later, 'Oh, look, Brenda darling, we've been photographed! No, of course I won't tell him our names if you'd rather not.'

'Here they come,' said Paul excitedly. 'Walter's still leading; aren't you thrilled, darling? Over the water jump, only one more now—over that—here they come—come on, Walter—come on, old boy—'

The horses thundered towards them, Walter leading easily. They approached the last fence, rose to it, Walter for some reason lost his balance and fell heavily to earth. Six horses in rapid succession jumped into the small of his back and passed on.

'You see,' said Walter that evening, as they settled down to bridge, 'the great advantage of getting blind before point-to-points. Sober I should certainly have been killed, as it is my left knee is a little sore but otherwise I feel grand.'

'The only thing is,' said Amabelle, 'that if you'd been a shade less drunk you might easily have won the race, instead of losing my five shillings in that careless way.'

'I should like to say that it's hardly the fault of anyone here if I'm not a widow to-night,' remarked Sally coldly. Major Stanworth, who had come, as he generally did now, to spend the evening at Mulberrie Farm, looked rather uncomfortable at this remark, which he took, and with reason, to be directed at himself.

17

It seemed to Philadelphia Bobbin that there was too much
going on in her life all at once, she had scarcely the time to
assimilate one new impression before being faced by another,
even stranger and more dazzlingly improbable than the last.
She felt a smouldering resentment against fate, which had
crowded three weeks of her ordinarily uneventful existence
with so many and such varying excitements. How much more
satisfactory if they could have been spread out over the
months and years of boredom which she had hitherto been
obliged to endure at Compton Bobbin. As things were, it was
in the course of three short weeks that she had fallen in love,
received a proposal of marriage, been precipitated into the
strange and dazzling society of Amabelle, and made friends
violently and passionately—'best friends', the kind of relationship that girls of her age have usually outgrown—with
Sally Monteath.

Any single one of these events would normally have kept
her happy and given her food for thought over a period of
months; crammed all together like this she was unable to treat
them as realities, but behaved rather as though the whole
thing were a play in a dream, and she the chief actress.

Philadelphia was twenty-one. She had hitherto led the flat,
uninspiring life of many such girls, 'educated' by a governess
(Lady Bobbin, for some reason about which she herself was
none too clear, disapproved of girls' schools), sent with the
same governess to Paris and Florence for six months, and then
'brought out' in London. Her mother took a house for her first
season in Eaton Place and escorted Philadelphia to dances
nearly every night in Pont Street, Chesham Place, Cadogan
Gardens, Queen's Gate or occasionally Hyde Park Gardens
or Sussex Square. Also she gave a dance for Philadelphia, for

which, the Eaton Place house being too small, she hired a large and dirty mansion in Belgrave Square.

All these dances were as one dance, absolutely and completely identical. Philadelphia, self-conscious and unhappy in her printed chiffon, her pink taffeta or her white and diamanté georgette, her hair too much crimped, her nose too much powdered and her stays much too tight (her beautiful rounded body being a constant source of worry to her) would follow Lady Bobbin, or some other chaperone on duty for the evening, up stairs already crowded to their utmost capacity into the noisy, hot and overwhelming ballroom. It then became her business to make herself agreeable to the young men who danced with her, because it was essential that when she met them in similar circumstances the next night and the night after they should be willing to repeat the experience. She soon realized that to sit in that silence for which alone she felt inclined until it was time to go back to the ballroom was merely to lay up for herself a future of wall-flowerdom, which fate she thought on the whole even more embarrassing and unamusing than that of attempting, usually in vain, to interest the nonentities in whose company she found herself. It was a fate, however, from which she did not entirely escape, despite all her efforts. She had no success in London, her beauty, as produced by Lady Bobbin, never appeared to its best advantage, and in any case was not such as would appeal to the heirs of Cadogan Place, while they were unallured by those long and indifferent silences, that complete absence of small talk which Paul and Michael were later to find so intriguing. Much, indeed, as she hated sitting, an obvious failure, by the wall with her mother, or a girl friend in like case, she was very little happier when perched on the back stairs or at the supper table with some strange man. Dancing she enjoyed; she was a beautiful dancer.

If her evenings were on the whole rather depressing, her days were made positively hideous by the girls' luncheon parties to which her mother forced her to go. 'You must get to know some nice girls; besides, as we are in London, I want you to do everything you are asked to. We need never come up

143

again.' Nearly every day, therefore, at one-thirty p.m., she would find herself in printed crêpe de chine, standing, finger pressed to bell marked 'Visitors', before some house in Pont Street, Chesham Place, Cadogan Gardens, Queen's Gate, Hyde Park Gardens or Sussex Square. She would be ushered into an empty L-shaped drawing-room decorated in the pre-pickled-wood-and-maps period, but brought slightly up-to-date by the presence of a waste-paper receptacle with an olde print stuck on to its plain green surface, a couple of Lalique ornaments and a pleated paper lampshade.

'I will tell Miss Joan (or Lady Felicity) that you are here, miss.' For Philadelphia, owing to early training, was one of those unfortunate people always fated to arrive a little before anybody else.

Presently Lady Joan (or Miss Felicity) would appear, and several pretty, fluffy girls in printed crêpe de chine and they would all go downstairs to a meal consisting of egg rissole with tomato sauce, cutlets with paper frills round the bone, hard round peas and new potatoes, followed by a pinkish jelly served in glasses with a tiny blob of cream on the top of each portion.

The conversation would run on the following lines:

'Which dance are you going to first to-night?'

'I think the Campbell-Parkers', because Archie said he'd meet me there, so I've booked up five and six with him. Besides, Lady Millicent Freke-Williams' is sure to be fearfully crowded at first.'

'I hear she's got thirty dinner parties for it.'

'I know. But I expect it will be fun later on. Which are you going to?'

'Well, I'm dining at the Freke-Williams' so I shall have to go there first, I suppose. Did you have fun last night? I was dying to get asked.'

'Yes, it was marvellous, but, my dear, the most awful thing happened. You see, Teddy asked me for number four and I said yes, and then Claud came up and said could he have number three or four because he had to go. Well, three was Johnny, and I never cut him; so I said "yes, four. But meet me

144

downstairs by the buffet, or else I shall be caught by Teddy."
So I went to the buffet at the beginning of number four and
waited for ages and Claud never came and Angela said she
had just seen him leave with Rosemary, so then I dashed
upstairs but Teddy had started dancing with Leila, so then,
my dear, I had to pick up that awful little Jamie Trent-
Pomeroy. I felt so ashamed at being seen with him. But wasn't
it awful of Claud—'

Philadelphia, meanwhile, would sit in a stony silence,
bored and boring, and when she had gone Lady Joan or Miss
Felicity would say to her girl friends, 'Isn't she too awful.
Mummy made me ask her.'

Philadelphia's one London season was from every point of
view a failure, and it had never, to her great relief, been
repeated. Lady Bobbin was far too much wrapped up in all
her country pursuits to leave them more than once for the
sake of a daughter who neither appreciated nor repaid such
sacrifice. She felt that she had done all that duty demanded
by the child, and could now rest on her laurels.

Philadelphia herself never had the slightest wish to repeat
that particular experience, but all the same she was
profoundly unhappy at Compton Bobbin. She was without
occupation or interest, the days dragged by each more boring
than the last, and she was beginning to think that perhaps she
was never to find those people who she felt sure must exist in
the world and who would prove more congenial to her than
those she had met as a débutante. She longed passionately for
even one friend who would not think her plain, stupid and
tongue-tied.

It is hardly surprising, therefore, if she was dazed and
incredulous on finding herself hailed as a beauty by
Amabelle, admitted to the confidences of Sally, treated as an
intellectual equal by Paul and asked in marriage by Michael,
all of whom were people she felt to be not only far more
intelligent and interesting than any she had met, but more
thrilling even than those imaginary beings whom, in day
dreams, she had longed to have as her friends.

All the attention and praise that she was now receiving had

the very natural effect of making her twice as pretty and attractive as she had been before, and with Sally to help and advise her she was even acquiring a certain chic.

'You're so lucky; you've got the sort of face that can be made into anything,' said Sally one day as they sat talking in Elspeth Paula's nursery. 'It's like a sheet of white paper waiting to be drawn on—or, at least, painted. The drawing's there all right; you've got beautiful features. Fancy having real natural platinum blonde hair, too; it's incredible. You'd have a wild success in London, you know.'

'I didn't when I went there.'

'No, of course not, with all those awful debs. I mean, among people who understand what real beauty is. You must come and stay in the flat when we go back there. We can easily make up a bed for you in the bathroom, or Amabelle will put you up, and then we'll arrange some parties. Now, I've got a very good idea: why not tell your mother you want to learn drawing and come to us permanently as P.G.? Do, it would be such fun.'

'Oh, Sally, you are divine to me, only, you see, I can't draw at all.'

'That doesn't matter. It makes a wonderful excuse to be in London. I can't draw a single line, and I was at the Slade for years. My family lived in the country, too, you see, and I had to get away somehow.'

'Mummy would never let me.'

'You and Bobby seem to be very much under your mother's thumb.'

'Yes, even Bobby's frightened of her, really, although he does pretend not to be. Besides, you see, all the money we have comes from her, and that puts her in a very strong position.'

'Yes, of course, I quite see that.'

Michael took Philadelphia for a walk and proposed to her by the statue of Apollo. It was, like everything that Michael did, very much stage managed, very well rehearsed, supremely diplomatic and in the last degree unimaginative. Nevertheless, had he arrived at Compton Bobbin three weeks earlier it is certain that Philadelphia would have accepted him on the spot; she longed for marriage, for escape from her home, which she regarded as a prison, and from her mother, whom she detested, and she had subconsciously imbibed enough of Bobby's somewhat outspoken snobbery to be not at all averse to the idea of being a rich marchioness. Even now, had he employed any other method of approach he would probably have been successful, as Philadelphia's feelings for Paul at this stage were hardly strong enough to outweigh the obvious advantages of marriage with Michael. Besides, she liked him very much.

They went for a long walk, during which he spoke in his cultured Foreign Office voice of his life in Egypt, and before that in Paris, and of his future prospects. Philadelphia, who had a sort of blind veneration for culture and learning in all forms, thought how charming he was and how lucky it was for her that at last she knew somebody who, just occasionally, in a way that never could bore, but quite perfectly, would insert into his speech some happy little quotation that she could often recognize, from various English poets, or even, though more rarely, a few words of Latin, French or German.

'So, you see,' he said, 'I intend to leave diplomacy now. As a career it has proved a great disappointment to me, I must own.'

Philadelphia, whose ideas on the Diplomatic Service were culled exclusively from the works of Maurice Baring and Marion Crawford, said that she had always imagined a diplomat's to be the most interesting life in the world.

'In theory I suppose it must be,' said Michael, 'because you see, in theory one would be in daily contact with the most important, most intelligent people of every nation, and that would be perfect. In practice one is continually being polite to elderly ladies in amethyst brooches, and that is not quite the same thing, is it? Although, I imagine that every life has its amethyst brooch side. All the same, I am inclined now to prefer the English variety to any other, so I am going to settle down at Lewes Park for good, with, perhaps, a *pied à terre* in Westminster from which I can attend, when I wish to do so, the House of Lords. I am told that a certain amount of good work is done there, even in these days, and of course it is very necessary that a few of the younger peers should take their seats,' he added complacently.

They walked in silence for a little. Presently Michael said:

'Here we are at this very exquisite statue of Apollo—I had quite forgotten its existence. How civilized, how charming, is it not? I wonder why Aunt Gloria allows it to be hidden by all these dreary shrubs. It is a perfect example of French eighteenth-century sculpture, and I should never be surprised if it turned out to be a genuine Bouchardon. Most satisfying—most.'

With a slight effort he removed his gaze from the statue and let it rest on Philadelphia's upturned face.

'I am going to ask you a question,' he said, 'and I don't want an answer until I get back from Lewes Park on Tuesday. I expect you can guess what it is going to be?'

'No,' said Philadelphia, honestly enough.

'I want you to marry me, my dear.'

She was as though turned to stone with amazement. Now was Michael's opportunity. If he had taken advantage of her surprise and obvious emotion to make love to her, Philadelphia, young, beautiful and longing to be loved, would probably have accepted him there and then. Unfortunately he had only given rein to his emotions with the one woman who would be alienated by that particular form of courtship, and he thought that he had now learnt his lesson once and for all. Women evidently disliked to be rushed off their feet, they must have time to make up their minds, sentiment in all forms was clearly anathema to them. So instead of taking her in his arms as of course he should have done there and then, he said coldly and rather shyly: 'Don't think of answering me now; you will have plenty of time to consider the matter during the next few days and you can let me know when I return. I feel sure that you will realize how very well suited we are to each other in every way, and indeed I would do my best to make you happy.' With that he embarrassed her rather by kissing her on the forehead, and they went indoors.

Philadelphia parted from him in the hall and ran upstairs to her bedroom. Her mind was in a state of excitement and confusion. She had never had a proposal of marriage before, and she was now thinking less of how she intended to answer Michael than of what she should do immediately and whom she could tell the grand news to. Deciding, as she powdered her nose, that it would be awkward to see Michael again before his departure, which was imminent, and that she must tell Sally first of anybody, she stole downstairs by the back way, got out her little car, and drove over to Mulberrie Farm.

She found Sally wheeling the baby up and down the gravel path. 'The little monster hasn't been asleep the whole afternoon,' she said. 'No, talking doesn't keep her awake; in fact, it seems to send her off, on the contrary. Your odious brother is in there, inducing Walter to waste his time and lose his money at bridge. It *is* so naughty of him. I know he's not written his weekly article yet, and it ought to have gone off by this post at the latest. I wish the game had never been invented.'

'Then who's the fourth?' asked Philadelphia, who knew that, except during week-ends, when Jerome came down from London, poor Sally was usually dragged in, much against her will, to play.

'Giles Stanworth, of course, my dear. He's never out of the house now, you know, night or day. The poor man's quite batty about Amabelle, and he's having to earn his keep by learning contract. Walter's taken a packet off him already, I may say.'

'Isn't it funny? I can't imagine Major Stanworth in love with anybody.'

'Can't you just! You wait till tea-time and then watch the way he goes on. It's pathetic. But the really extraordinary thing is that I believe Amabelle rather fancies him too, I honestly think she does. Yesterday evening—' Sally broke off. She was a very discreet person where her friends were concerned, and decided that for the present she would keep the doings of yesterday evening to herself. 'I dare say we shall

149

see the old girl a farmer's wife yet,' she added hastily to cover her lapse. 'What news from Compton Bobbin?'

'Michael's motoring back to Lewes after tea.'

'He is, is he? That's no great loss anyway. I shouldn't think anyone will miss him unbearably—I never notice whether he's about or not myself, do you?'

'Not much,' said Philadelphia, rather dashed by this remark. She feared that Sally would be unimpressed by her news. There was a short silence. 'He proposed to me before he left,' she said at last.

'Delphie! You don't say so? My dear, isn't that *grand*. When are you going to announce it? Oh, you lucky girl.'

'Oh, I haven't said yes. I mean I haven't given him any answer yet, you see. I'm to think it over until he comes back.'

'But of course you'll accept, won't you?'

'I hadn't thought so. I'm not in love with him.'

'My darling Delphie, you mustn't *hesitate*. Michael is a divine person. We all adore him; he's quite perfect in every way. Attractive, intelligent, everything you could want in the world. Besides just think of all that money. Why, you could afford to have ten children if you liked.'

'That would be nice,' said Philadelphia doubtfully; 'but you see I'm not in love with him.'

'Nonsense, of course you are. One couldn't help being in love with a heavenly person like that if he wanted one to be. Besides, nobody is in love with their husbands before they marry, at least I was, but that's most exceptional. It's hardly ever done. You're not fancying anyone else, by the way, are you?'

'I don't know.'

'Of course you're not.' Sally looked relieved. 'Well, that's too lovely, darling, I do congratulate you. I wonder where you'll be married, Westminster Abbey, perhaps. Shall we go and tell the others? No, no, not unless you like, of course, but I'll tell Amabelle afterwards as a great secret, can I? And you wouldn't be an angel, I suppose, and let me sell it to the press (I mean when it's all quite settled, naturally), because I could get at least a tenner for the news, do let me have it and not

Bobby, please. How gorgeous of you, isn't it? I wonder what sort of ring he'll be giving you. You are a lucky girl, Delphie, I must say.'

After Sally had been working on her mind in this manner for about half an hour, Philadelphia began to regard herself quite as the future Lady Lewes, doubts and misgivings faded from her mind and she felt already a delightful new sense of her own importance. If Sally, whom she looked up to in every way, thought that it would be all right for her to marry Michael she herself would raise no further objections. Indeed, Sally had done Michael's own work for him most efficiently, and by the time that they had discussed every aspect of the wedding, from the cheering crowds outside the Abbey to the pattern of nightdress for her trousseau, Philadelphia was feeling quite romantic about him. She had some difficulty at tea-time in keeping the news to herself, and even threw out one or two hints at a mystery to which she alone had a clue, but nobody paid much attention to her. They were all busy watching the latest developments in the situation between Mrs. Fortescue and Major Stanworth.

When Philadelphia returned to Compton Bobbin she found a note from Michael on the hall table.

'MY DEAREST PHILADELPHIA,

'I couldn't find you anywhere to say good-bye. However, I shall be back again in less than a week (next Tuesday at the very latest, D.V.), and shall expect my answer then. Consider the matter very carefully, my dear, remembering that marriage is a state which once entered into, lasts the whole of one's life. I need hardly say how much I hope that you will consent to be my wife, and I truly believe that in trusting me with your future happiness you will be putting it into reliable hands. I spoke of this before I left to Aunt Gloria. Remember, dearest Philadelphia, that if you are in any doubt as to how you should act, there can be no one so well fitted to guide and advise you as your own mother.

'with love from
MICHAEL.'

This peculiar missive probably seemed less chilling to Philadelphia, who had never in her life before received a love letter, than it would have to most girls of twenty-one. On the other hand, it certainly did not arouse in her those emotions which the loved handwriting is usually supposed to evoke, and the reference to Lady Bobbin annoyed her a good deal.

Michael went to Lewes Park to settle up certain matters with his estate agent. He intended to stay there under a week. The day after he arrived, however, he caught a chill which developed into jaundice and kept him in bed for nearly a month. This circumstance very nearly altered the entire course of his life.

Before leaving Compton Bobbin he had an interview with his Aunt Gloria, during which he informed her of his intentions and hopes with regard to Philadelphia. Lady Bobbin was, of course, delighted.

'My dear Michael,' she said, almost with emotion, 'this is the best news I could possibly have. How pleased poor Hudson would have been, too. We will discuss the business side of it another time—I have to go now and speak to the huntsman about a new horse—but I may as well tell you that I have always intended to settle £2,000 a year on Philadelphia if she marries with my approval, and of course when I die she will be fairly well off. I must rush away now, so good-bye, and we meet again on Tuesday?'

'Of course she hasn't accepted me for certain yet,' said Michael with more than a touch of complacency, 'but I may say that I have little doubt that all will be well in that direction. Good-bye, then, Aunt Gloria, thank you so much for my delightful visit.'

Philadelphia herself came back from Mulberrie Farm with her mind quite made up. Sally's way of treating the whole thing as an accomplished fact had made her feel that it was so, and she only wished that Michael had not gone away and that they could begin all the exciting business, as outlined by Sally, of being engaged that very evening. She decided to answer his letter at once, begging him to return as soon as he could, and was going towards the schoolroom with this object in view when she ran into her mother.

'Oh, Philadelphia, come in here a minute. I want to speak to you. Well, darling, Michael has told me your news and I am, I need hardly say, quite delighted. It is far the best thing that could possibly have happened, and we shall be able to announce your engagement at the dance I am giving the day before Bobby goes back to Eton.'

Lady Bobbin had the somewhat unfortunate effect upon both her children of invariably provoking them to argument.

'But I haven't any intention of marrying Michael,' said Philadelphia defiantly. 'He proposed to me, certainly, but I never accepted him.'

'Then I hope that you will do so without delay,' said Lady Bobbin acidly. 'Michael spoke to me as though it was all settled.'

'He may have settled it, but I haven't.'

'You really are a very silly obstinate little girl. Michael will make you a most ideal husband. Surely you like him, don't you? What is it you have against him?'

'Yes, I like him all right, except that I think he's rather a pompous old thing,' said Philadelphia, a phrase she had borrowed from Bobby.

'Nonsense. Michael has a very proper sense of duty, of the responsibilities attached to his position in the world, and I am very glad that he has. You don't want a sort of clown and buffoon for a husband. And in any case, if you don't marry him you'll probably remain an old maid, I should think. I can't imagine that you will ever find anybody else half so suitable or so nice. And I may as well tell you, Philadelphia, while we are on this subject, that I am not obliged to settle a penny of money on you if you marry without my approval.'

'All right,' said Philadelphia sulkily, 'I'll think about it.' She left the room, tearing up Michael's letter into small pieces as she went.

In the schoolroom she found Paul, whom she had hardly seen all day.

'Your grandmother was most certainly a genius,' he said, looking up from the Journal, 'although in some respects her character was not everything that could have been wished for. But her prose seems to me even to transcend her poetry in literary merit, and her metaphysical conclusions are always faultless. Listen to this now:

'One curious and very noticeable feature of the workings of a human mind is that so often it will seize upon and stress the unimportant almost to the exclusion of anything else. This it does most especially in dreams. Last night, for example, I dreamt that I was playing in the nursery with darling Julia when, suddenly seizing her teddy-bear, which I gave her yesterday and which cost me 4s. 6d. in the Baker Street Bazaar, she flung herself upon the blazing fire and was burnt to a cinder. In the dream (and this illustrates my point) I was worried far less by the extinction of poor Julia than by that of the bear, and I wandered about saying very sorrowfully, "It was a four-and-sixpenny bear".'

'Funny reading that just now,' Paul went on, 'because last night I had just such a dream myself. Would you like to hear it?'

Philadelphia stifled the feeling of acute boredom which comes over those about to hear the dreams of others, and said that she would.

'Well, it was a very odd dream indeed. You and I and Michael were going down to Brighton for the wedding of the Prince Regent to Mrs. Fitzherbert. We took first-class return tickets. But when we arrived at the Pavilion, where the wedding was to be held, we found that all the people there were French, and dressed in clothes of the time of Louis XIV, and Michael was very much put out by this. He said to me, loudly and angrily, "This is really too much. These people to begin with are not English, most of them don't know the Regent, even by sight, and they haven't had the common decency to dress in the proper clothes of the period. Besides, Sheridan isn't here, and Mrs. Fitzherbert has gone off to the Y.W.C.A. in a rage. I don't blame her, I must say, but I do feel annoyed that we have been dragged all the way down here, first-class for nothing." So we all came straight back to London, first-class.

'Now in the whole of that dream, which was long and quite involved, I was only really impressed by one important fact, which was that we travelled first-class. I woke up with the words "first-class" on my lips, and can still, although the rest of the dream has practically faded from my mind, see most clearly in my imagination the upholstered seats with arms, clean white lace antimacassars and little views of Bath and Wells in our first-class carriage.'

'Very strange,' said Philadelphia, burning the pieces of Michael's letter. Life itself, she thought, as she went upstairs to dress for dinner, was stranger than dreams and far, far more disordered.

18

'Jerome,' said Amabelle.

Jerome looked up from his weekly, rather shamefaced, perusal of *The Tatler*.

'Yes, Amabelle?'

'I've got some news to tell you.'

'What's that, my dear?'

'I'm going to marry Giles Stanworth.'

'Oh, my God,' said Jerome, and buried his face in his hands.

'Amabelle—it isn't true, is it?' he said, a minute later; 'you don't really mean it, do you?'

'Yes, you know, it's quite true. The banns are going to be called to-morrow in the village church—not in this village, because Giles says the parson here is really a papist, but in Hogrush. It's jolly exciting, don't you think? We're being married at the beginning of February, down here. I shall wear a hat, of course, and we both hope that you'll give me away, darling.'

'I shall do no such thing.'

'Then Bobby will have to.'

'Are you off your head, Amabelle? I really never heard such scandalous nonsense in all my life. Only think of that poor man dragged up to Portman Square, out of his element, wretched, bored—'

'I don't think of it for a moment. Giles would never leave his precious farm, not even for me; besides, I shouldn't ask him to. I'm looking forward to living in the country myself.'

'My dear, you are being a little bit childish, aren't you?'

'No, darling, not in the least. However, I suppose I had better explain the situation to you quite clearly, then perhaps you'll see my point of view for once. First of all, then, I happen to be very fond of Giles, and I adore his little boy.'

'If you're so anxious to be married, why not marry Michael?'

'Because Michael bores me into fits, and I don't like being laughed at by my friends and acquaintances. People always laugh when a woman marries someone fifteen years younger than herself, quite right, too.'

'I don't understand why you want to marry at all. Aren't you happy?'

'If you would listen to me for one single minute—'

'Oh, all right, go on.'

'The real point is, old boy, that I am forty-five. You didn't know that, did you? Still, there it is. Now what happens to women like me, unattached but not unattractive women, when they are over forty-five? It's very tricky, I can tell you. They gradually begin to get taken up by boys at Oxford, who rather like being seen about with them and all that, but who really regard them as a cross between a fortune-teller, a nanny, and an interesting historical character who has somehow managed to live on until the present day. I've seen it happen over and over again, haven't you, honestly? And at about fifty-five or so people start saying, "How *wonderful* Amabelle looks for her age. Of course she must be well over seventy now, why, when I was a girl she was quite an old woman." It's an awful, and, as far as I can see, an inevitable fate, and it seems to me more dignified to retire before it overtakes one.'

'I think you are wrong,' said Jerome. 'You have been feeling depressed, I suppose, and no wonder in this ghastly house, but that is no reason for making such a terrible mistake. You'll be miserable, bored and miserable living down here always. Giles Stanworth is very nice, of course, I think he is charming, but what interests have you in common?'

'The Fluke, for one. You wouldn't believe how passionately I am interested in the Fluke. There is another fascinating disease called the staggers too, he tells me; horses have that. Then the rotation of crops—'

'Can't you be serious for one minute?' cried Jerome in

exasperation. 'I see nothing to joke about in the fact that you are jeopardizing your whole future happiness for a crazy idea like this. Look here, Amabelle, if you must marry, marry me.'

'Darling Jerome, you *are* sweet. But what would Mrs. Nickle say?' Mrs. Nickle had been Jerome's housekeeper for twenty years. 'No, no, my dear, that would never do. Besides, strange though it may seem to you, I actually do want to marry Giles; and as nothing that you can say will stop me you might just as well look pleasant and wish me happiness.'

'I may be dense, but I still don't see the point in taking this step. It's no good pretending to me that you are passionately in love with Giles Stanworth, or anything so silly as that.'

'Actually I am rather in love with him. But that's neither here nor there. The point, as I've told you already, is that I don't want to be taken up by Oxford undergraduates.'

'I think you exaggerate the danger of these youths, the modern young man is not quite so importunate as perhaps you may imagine.'

'No, that's just it, one wouldn't mind so much if he were. It's the maiden aunt relationship that I object to more than anything.'

'You're incorrigible, Amabelle.'

'Pig-headed, you mean. Anyhow, you might wish me luck, old boy.'

'I do—I do. Oh, how bored you'll be after about six months of country life.'

'You said that before, if you remember, when I took this house. Actually I was at first, terribly bored for about a day, but since then I've enjoyed myself top-hole.'

'For a few weeks, yes. You've had people to amuse you and so on. But think of months and years on that awful farm.'

'It isn't awful at all. It's a sweet little house. I think I shall adore being a farmer's wife. I intend to have a still room and make my own face creams out of herbs, and Giles has lent me a book of sillabubs and flummery caudles and all sorts of art and craft food, and did you know before that ye rhubarbe maketh to go to ye privy? I bet you didn't.'

The news of Amabelle's engagement spread like wildfire

after the banns had been read out in church the following Sunday. Bobby came round in a state of high excitement, and after kissing her repeatedly he said to Major Stanworth:

'Amabelle has always been in love with me really, of course, and that's why she's going to marry you, simply in order to live near Compton Bobbin. Darling, darling, you ought to have seen mummy's face in church! She said afterwards, "Poor Giles, I must say I never imagined that he would end up by marrying a woman of the demimonde, but I suppose she has got him into her clutches like so many others. It will be a finisher for him.""

Major Stanworth got rather red. Although by his own lights he was an exceptionally broadminded man, he never could quite accustom himself to hearing Amabelle's friends refer in this light-hearted way to her past.

'You heard what mother said to Auntie Loudie,' went on the tactless child. 'You see apparently she found out somehow that I know you quite well, and she was talking it over with Auntie Loudie, who was divine as usual, and said nothing matters for boys in that sort of way, and mother agreed with her more or less, and finally she said, "Anyhow I am told it costs £10,000 to sleep with Mrs. Fortescue, so I suppose it's all right for Bobby to go over there sometimes."'

'Your mother can't know much about the state of the market in these days,' observed Amabelle drily.

'However, she said at lunch that she will receive you when you're married for Giles' sake, because she always stands by her friends in their misfortunes. It's one of her boasts, like changing for dinner in the bush—she's white all through, my mother is. And she's going to the wedding with the whole hunt, they'll meet at the church and play "gone to ground" over you on the horn and everything. It will be a riot, won't it?'

'Won't it just?' said Amabelle delightedly. 'Will you be able to get away from Eton for it, my sweet?'

'Well, I've been thinking about that. May I be best man? Then they'll simply have to give me leave.'

'No, you may not,' said Giles Stanworth.

159

19

'I love you, I love you, I love you, I love you, I love you, I love you, I love you, I love you,' said Paul. 'I love you. And if there were anything more to say I should say it, but there isn't, really.'

'Oh, isn't there just,' said Philadelphia rather tartly, drawing herself to the other end of the sofa and smoothing down her ruffled hair. 'Personally, I should have thought there was a good deal more that you might have said by now.'

'That only shows that you don't love me as much as I love you, my sweet poppet.'

'Yes, I do. Much more, as a matter of fact.'

'What makes you think that?'

'For one thing I've never loved anybody in my life before.'

'Nor have I.'

'What about Marcella then?'

'Oh, Marcella! She never meant a thing to me, not a thing. I thought she was rather attractive, but as for loving her—'

'And Susan and Elizabeth and Sheila and Sonia and Rosemary and Joan and Veronica?'

'Sally's been talking to you. I think it's very naughty and horrid of her. I promise you I never cared for any of those girls in the way I care for you. No other woman will ever be the same to me, you're something quite special in my life, quite apart.'

'Well, I believe you, darling, though I expect it's very silly of me to, and you must see it's a risk I'm taking. In any case, it's time we began to think of what we're going to do next.'

'Darling, don't be so practical. Everything will be all right in the end, I promise you it will, only don't fuss.'

'But I am fussing. Here we've been engaged for two whole days, and you've done nothing about it except to kiss me on

160

the sofa and tell me lies about other girls you've been in love with.'

'But, my darling, what d'you expect me to do?'

'I expect you to take steps.'

'What steps?'

'Oh, you are maddening.'

'Yes, but really, what steps? I'm going to marry you, my precious, and that's taking a big step, I should have thought.'

'Marry me!' cried Philadelphia in despair. 'I know, so you say, but how—how—how? How are you going to tell mother, how do you intend to support me; above all, how am I to get disengaged from Michael? You don't seem to realize that if he hadn't caught jaundice, by the mercy of Providence, he would have been back again yesterday, ring and all.'

'I can see quite plainly that you've been talking about this to Sally,' said Paul sulkily, 'and if it goes on I shall be obliged to tell your mother that as soon as her back is turned you are off like greased lightning to Mulberrie Farm. She'll soon put a stop to that.'

'Paul, darling, do you love me?'

'Yes, I do.'

'Then go and tell mother that we're engaged.'

'I'm going to, to-morrow morning.'

'You said that yesterday.'

'I know I did. I felt so awful this morning that I simply couldn't face it. There were brains for breakfast again, and the sight of them always upsets me. But to-morrow I'm going to be brave and heroic. And you're going to write to Michael, aren't you, and I'm going to write a best-seller about your great-grandmother, and we shall be as happy as the day is long, you'll see. So give me a kiss and stop bothering, won't you?'

'No, I won't. Will you go and tell mother this evening as soon as she comes in from hunting?'

'Darling, please not. You don't know the effect your mother has on my nerves; it's positively uncanny. I shiver and shake like an aspirin leaf, whatever that may be.'

'Have a whisky and soda first.'

161

'That wouldn't really do. Supposing she smelt my breath, like the police in motor accidents?'

'Well, when do you intend to tell her?'

'Darling, you're not being just a shade governessy, are you? If you really want to know, I don't see very much point in telling her at all. It will only mean that I shall have to leave by the next train if I do. Imagine my position. "Oh, Lady Bobbin, by the way, my name is Fotheringay, not Fisher, and I've been here all this time under false pretences, and I've never done a stroke of work with Bobby, but instead I've been collecting material for the life you don't want me to write of Lady Maria, and I should like to marry your daughter, but as I haven't any money I should be glad if you would pay off just a few of my more pressing debts and buy me a tail coat to be married in as I've rather grown out of my old Eton one." It doesn't sound too well, you know.'

'Oh, Paul, whatever are we to do?'

'"The glory of man is in being, not in doing."'

Philadelphia burst into angry tears.

'Don't cry now, darling. Everything will be all right, you'll see.'

'Let's go and ask Amabelle what she thinks, shall we?'

'Oh, very well, if you like. Anything to stop you crying. Not that I imagine she'll be much good to us, but still—'

They found Amabelle wringing her hands in front of the drawing-room fire at Mulberrie Farm. There was a strong smell of bananas in the room.

'It's all right,' she said. 'This is not a sign of mental anguish. Giles hasn't given me the raspberry or anything like that. I've just been varnishing my nails, and I simply can't get them to dry.' And she fell to wringing her hands with even greater vigour than before. 'I wanted particularly to see you, Philadelphia. Walter and Sally left for the south of France yesterday in a wild hurry. Someone was paying for them, and the poor sweets think it will cost them nothing. Sally was miserable she couldn't say good-bye, and left a thousand messages. They're only going for a couple of weeks, but you see they won't be coming back here again as I'm off to

162

London myself on Saturday to buy my trousseau, dear, for the farm. I think of having corduroy trousers like the ones that Giles wears; they ought to be quite attractive. Lucky I've kept my figure, isn't it? Where's Bobby, by the way?'

'He's staying with Bunch for a shoot; he'll be back to-morrow.'

'Send him along, will you? I want to see him before I go. I don't suppose I shall get out of it under a fiver, but still. *What* it will save me in tips when that child goes to Oxford.'

'Amabelle, we really came to ask your advice about something.'

'Oh, did you just?'

'Paul and I are engaged to be married.'

'I know; Sally told me. You don't expect me to congratulate you or anything like that, do you?'

'I think you're being rather unkind; it's nearly always done, isn't it? And anyway, why not?'

'Because it is no matter for congratulations, my poor sweet. I suppose you think you are in love with each other?'

'We don't think it. We are in love,' said Paul defiantly. He had an idea of what Amabelle was going to say next.

'Then how can I possibly congratulate you? You must both know quite well that this marriage is practically an impossibility. At the best you have endless fusses and bothers in front of you; Lady Bobbin will, very naturally, refuse to give you any money. Paul has nothing but debts, you will both have to be terribly worried and unhappy for ages before you can be married, and miserably poor, probably for years, afterwards. Not a very enchanting prospect, to my mind.'

'Look how poor Walter and Sally are,' said Philadelphia. 'They couldn't be worse off, but they are the two happiest people I've ever seen.'

'Walter and Sally are very exceptional. I am inclined even to think that they are unique; anyhow, I personally have never come across another case like theirs in my life. Nothing that could happen would ever make the smallest difference to their feeling for each other. I suppose a love of that sort can be found once in a generation. I don't want to seem unkind, because I am very fond of you both, but I very much doubt whether either you or Paul has the character which is needed to sustain such a relationship—you won't believe me, of course. It's a funny thing that people are always quite ready to admit it if they've no talent for drawing or music, whereas everyone imagines that they themselves are capable of true love, which is a talent like any other, only far more rare. I don't doubt, mind you, that if Paul were an eligible young man and if you could be married in the usual way without any trouble, you would probably be quite happy. I only say that as things are it's impossible.'

'Oh, Amabelle,' cried Philadelphia, 'unkind, unkind! I thought that you at least would be able to advise us.'

'If you really want my advice here it is, but you won't like it much. Don't say a word to anybody; don't let your mother or Bobby suspect a thing, but have a lovely time together till next week, when Paul is going away in any case. Then, as soon as Michael has finished having jaundice, announce your engagement to him. Please believe me when I say that you'll be very happy with him. I know Michael so well and I feel sure of it. He'll take you for a gorgeous honeymoon, all round the world perhaps, and when you get back you'll settle down at that exquisite Lewes Park and have some nice babies, and entertain a lot, and be the best-dressed marchioness in England. I don't know how you can hesitate, I really don't.'

Philadelphia began to cry again.

'Thank you for nothing,' said Paul loudly and angrily. 'Look how you've upset my poor darling Delphie. Don't cry, my precious; you shan't marry that old bore, he'd drive you mad in a week. I thought at least you would have shown us some sympathy, Amabelle, but I suppose it's too much to expect even that. You women are all the same, a lot of blasted matchmakers, that's what you are.'

'Paul, Paul, don't be so bitter. You must have known that I of all people would take the common sense point of view. Just think for a moment; use your intelligence, my dear. You and Philadelphia have known each other for exactly three weeks. You both think, honestly I'm sure, that you are ready to undergo almost intolerable hardships over a period of years, and possibly for life, in order to be able to remain in each other's company. I say that it would be much easier, more to your mutual advantage and eventual happiness, if you could bring yourselves to part now and lead different lives. That's all.'

'Of course,' said Philadelphia, sniffing rather loudly, 'my mother would probably give us some sort of allowance once we were actually married; she'd be obliged to, really.'

'I doubt it very much,' said Amabelle; 'from what I know of your mother's character I should think it most unlikely. At present she naturally wishes you to marry Michael; when you tell her of your engagement to Paul she will be furious, and doubly so when she discovers the trick that has been played on her all this time. Think of her feelings when you tell her that he is not only not Mr. Fisher, but actually that Mr. Fotheringay whom she refused to have in the house!'

'Yes, that's awful, I must say,' said Paul.

'And what will happen? Angry words will pass of the sort that can never, never be forgotten, and you will find yourselves faced with the alternative of eloping on the spot and living on Paul's £300 a year' (Amabelle had an amazing faculty for knowing to a penny the incomes of her friends) 'or of staying at home and leading an incredibly drab and dreary life, more or less in disgrace with your mother, until he can make enough money to support you in moderate comfort, which, as far as I can see, will be never.'

'Oh, God!' said Paul.

'I'm sorry to be so depressing, but I say again, for heaven's sake, marry Michael. If you don't I see nothing but trouble ahead for you, my poor Philadelphia.'

'Now listen to me, Amabelle,' said Philadelphia, with unexpected firmness. 'I am not going to marry Michael, and I *am* going to marry Paul. Get that clear, and then tell me what I ought to do about it.'

Amabelle frowned. She was incapable of seeing Philadelphia's point of view, and thought that the child was being merely obstinate.

'Thank heaven I haven't got a daughter,' she said impatiently. 'However, if you really mean what you say, I consider there is only one course open to you. Refuse Michael, giving no reason for doing so, keep all this a deadly secret (and by that I mean a secret—no hints or half-confessions to anybody, you understand) and wait for a few months while Paul finds some good, steady job. Then let Bobby go to your mother, tell her the whole story and ask her to give you enough money to be married; he is much more likely to get round her than you are, I imagine. By then she will have lost all hope of Michael as a son-in-law and may be quite anxious to get you off, even to somebody as ineligible as Paul. Only it's essential that he should first get a proper job and keep it for a few months. That seems to me your only possible hope. And of course, Paul, it goes without saying that you must give up the idea of publishing Lady Maria's life, anyhow, until you have got a good marriage settlement tucked away.'

Paul and Philadelphia looked glum. The prospect of a glamorous elopement was far more attractive to them than a course of action which necessitated on his part the daily grind of some regular job, so long and so studiously avoided by him, and on hers the indefinite continuation of her present dreary life. However, they could not but admit that this was the most sensible course to follow, and both felt immensely relieved that it would not, at present, be necessary to beard Lady Bobbin in her den.

'Thank you, dear Amabelle,' said Philadelphia. 'I think you are quite right, although it will be terrible to wait all that time. Still, it won't be so bad when you come to live here for good.'

'Of course not,' said Amabelle cheerfully. 'I'll have Paul to stay every week-end, and I expect Walter and Sally will be down sometimes, so it won't be nearly as lonely for you at Compton Bobbin as it used to be. All the same, I think you're making a terrible mistake, my dear, in refusing Michael. I shall never alter my opinion about that.'

Paul said, as they walked back to Compton Bobbin, 'I'll tell you what I'll do. My Uncle Joseph has some ghastly sort of business in the city. I'll make him give me a job, he has offered to before. I see what Amabelle means; your mother is far more likely to come round to the idea of our marriage if she thinks I have definite work. People of that generation are so extraordinary in those ways; they don't care about self-expression or any of the things that really matter. So long as one has a good solid and respectable job they are quite satisfied about one. The truth is that they have misused leisure themselves for so long that they think of it as a bad thing for anybody to have. Never mind, I will crucify myself for your sake, sweet one, on an office stool, for a month or two anyway, until we see what happens. Something is sure to turn up, it always does. It's a bit souring about Lady Maria all the same. I was looking forward to publishing that.'

'Darling, I hate to think of you making such a sacrifice.'

'There's no sacrifice I wouldn't make for you, darling. Besides, the moment we're married I shall bring it out and show the world that I'm a serious writer of the front rank.'

'Paul, I do love you.'

'Darling, darling Philadelphia. How do you manage to be so heavenly with a mother like that?'

'I believe daddy was rather sweet.'

'That accounts for it then, no doubt.'

As soon as Bobby got back from his shoot he went round to see Amabelle.

'What's all this nonsense about Paul and Delphie?' he said accusingly.

'Oh, so you know about it by now, do you? Who told you?'

'Nobody told me, but I should have to be as dense as my mother seems to be if I couldn't see with half an eye what's happening. They sit holding hands on the drawing-room sofa all day, and Delphie keeps on throwing out dark hints about how wonderful it is to be in love and all that sort of thing. It can only be a matter of moments now before mummy tumbles to it, I should think, and then there'll be the devil to pay.'

'Didn't I know those silly children would never be able to

keep it quiet? And what view do you take of the whole thing, Bobby? You needn't tell me, darling. I can guess.'

'Well, naturally, I think it's quite crazy. I only hope and pray that Delphie won't ruin her chances of marrying Michael by her idiocy, that's all. Thank heaven he's out of the way for the present. As for Paul, I really do think it's a bit hard he should behave like this after all the trouble I've taken for him.'

'I must say I agree with you for once,' said Amabelle. 'They came over yesterday to confess it all and ask my advice, and I'm afraid I was rather unkind to them. I've seen Paul wildly in love with too many people to take that very seriously, and as for Philadelphia, why at her age one is in love every other week. I gather that Michael made a mess of everything as usual. He had only to go about it with a little ordinary sense and she'd have been crazy about him by now. Really that young man, I've no patience at all with him; he behaves like a very unconvincing character in a book, not like a human being at all.'

'Yes, doesn't he. The sort of book of which the reviewers would say "the characterization is weak; the central figure, Lord Lewes, never really coming to life at all; but there are some fine descriptive passages of Berkshire scenery." What did you say to Delphie?'

'I told her she was mad not to marry Michael, and then she began to cry, and I really hadn't the heart to go on. I finally told them that if they intend to marry in spite of everything they must keep this affair a deadly secret until Paul has some satisfactory job. Of course they'll do neither the one thing nor the other. They are evidently not capable of keeping a secret, and I can no more imagine Paul in a job than a fly.'

'Good gracious, no; he'd never stick to it for a day.'

'I suppose, in point of fact, that if they did marry your mother would have to give them some sort of allowance, but it's much better that they shouldn't think so, because Paul, who must, after all, have a good idea of what poverty means, isn't likely to elope with her unless he can be fairly certain that there will be some money eventually.'

'Paul's not mercenary, you know,' said Bobby.

'Not in the least, but he's not an absolute fool either. I doubt if he'd risk such a thing, for her sake as well as his own. The worst of it is that I don't believe, apart from the money side of it, that they would be particularly happy together. They are really most unsuited. Paul needs somebody who is very strong-minded and who will manage him. Why, even that repellent girl, Marcella, would be a better wife for him. As for Philadelphia, the darling, she is obviously cut out to have money and position.'

'And I shall do my very best to see that she gets both,' said Bobby with one of his self-conscious smiles. 'What a fund of common sense you are, darling. You've cheered me up enormously. What is my line for the moment, then?'

'You must do all you can to keep this nonsense a secret from your mother. If she finds out it will be fatal. She'll probably say a lot of bitter and unkind things to both of them and as likely as not drive them straight into an elopement. If it can be kept from her I give the whole thing three months at the most before it fizzles out.'

'That ought to be easy. Paul goes away in less than a week now, when I trail back to the old col., and mother is still out hunting most of the time. Besides, several people are coming to stay here over the week-end for this bogus dance she will insist on having. I dare say she won't notice anything much; she's been as blind as a bat so far.'

'We can only hope for the best,' said Amabelle, who was looking out of the window. 'Hullo, here comes my fiancé—whatever is he carrying? Oh, I say, isn't that rather sweet, d'you see; he's bringing two dead hens for the kitchen; he always has some exquisite present for me, the angel.'

'Well, I'll be off,' said Bobby, rather sourly; 'and I don't suppose, if you're really going to London, that I shall see you again until after you're married, which is too awful. Look here, darling, will you promise to go and choose yourself a present at Cartier? I've got an account there, so get something really nice, won't you, not a diamond hen, though, if you don't mind.'

20

The dance at Compton Bobbin was in no way a riot of joyous and abandoned merriment; it was, in fact, even more dreary an entertainment than might have been anticipated, and was long afterwards remembered by Cotswold beaux and belles as 'that frightful party at the Bobbins'. When the guests arrived, cold and dazzled after a long motor drive, they found neither the cheering strains of Terpsichore nor the sustaining draught of Bacchus awaiting them. The young man from Woodford who had been engaged to provide the former came very late indeed, so that for quite half-an-hour the guests stood about in uncertain groups, while Paul and Squibby struggled to make the wireless work. When finally he did arrive, breathless and apologetic, having left his car upside down in a ditch, his playing proved to be of that sort which induces sleep rather than revelry by night. Lady Bobbin had remained true to her resolution that in *her* house there should be no champagne during the national crisis, and on every hand could soon be heard the groans and curses with which British youth greets the absence of any alcohol more fortifying than beer at its parties. The rare and somewhat tipsy appearances downstairs of Bobby, the duchess, and such of their intimates as were secretly invited to the cocktail bar provided by Bobby in his bedroom, merely accentuated the wretched sobriety of the other guests.

The duchess and Héloïse were staying with Bunch for this occasion, as also were Squibby, Biggy and Maydew. The two latter, however, had most ungallantly refused to attend the dance, giving as their excuse that they always felt sick in motor cars. Everybody else was quite well aware that they really wished to stay at home in order to play Brahms on two pianos. As a result of this monstrous behaviour the girls who had been invited by Bunch solely on their behalf spent the greater part of the evening sitting drearily together in the hall. This fact appeared to weigh rather on the duchess, who, as their chaperone, felt that she ought to feel some responsibility for their amusement.

'Those wretched girls,' she kept saying, in the intervals of helping Bobby to mix the cocktails, 'oughtn't I to do something about them? Shall we have them up here, darling?'

'Oh, don't let's. They look so gloomy, and there's hardly enough drink to go round as it is. Anyways, I expect they enjoy being together down there.'

'Of course they don't; they look furious, and I don't blame them either. I think it's simply odious of Biggy and Maydew to get them asked down and then stay behind like that. If I were Lady Tarradale I should be quite furious, especially as they're certain to keep her awake all night with their awful music, and she's been so wretchedly ill lately. Those poor charming girls, looking so sweet in their pink and green, too. I do feel badly about them. Do go and see if they're all right, Bobby, won't you?'

'Darling, you know they're not all right, so why bother? Besides, they're Bunch's guests, not mine. Let him look after them.'

'Bunch has got his own girl here, Sonia Beckett. You can't expect him to do more than dance about once with each of the others. Hullo, Héloïse, darling. Come here, sweetest, I want to whisper. Angel, is it quite necessary for you to wander about with four young men when poor Rosemary and Laetitia have no one at all to talk to them?'

'I don't think anyone wants to talk to them,' said Héloïse; 'they're such cracking bores, aren't they? Give me a cocktail, darling, quickly. This party is quite the bloodiest I've ever been to, personally. How right Biggy and Maydew were to stay behind. I do envy them, don't you?'

'Squibby dear,' said the duchess, waving an empty glass at Bobby as she spoke, 'just tell me something. Have you seen

Rosemary and Laetitia latishly? Are they all right, the sweet poppets?'

'Oh, yes,' said the heartless Squibby. 'I expect so. Sure to be. I saw them having a very jolly little chat with Lady Prague just now.'

'You don't think it would be rather nice if you went and saw how they were getting on?'

'Well, Aunt Loudie, I don't think I need. I'd much rather stay and talk to you. In any case, I've danced with both of them and they are nothing to do with me. It was Biggy and Maydew who insisted on having them asked down.'

Paul and Philadelphia spent most of the evening shut up together in the linen cupboard, bemoaning the fact that tomorrow they must be parted, and reiterating that they intended to be faithful to each other during the months to come.

'Darling, when I think,' said Philadelphia, her voice shaking, 'of all those lovely girls you go out with in London I do feel so terrified that you'll soon forget all about me.'

'I shan't do that. I tell you that you have quite a special place in my heart, and you always will have. Wherever I am I shall be thinking about you the whole time. I expect I shall go about with other girls, because it would be a mistake not to, but they won't mean anything to me really. You are, and always will be, the only woman in my life. I shall never feel about anybody as I do about you. You're perfect, to me.'

The fact that Paul had repeated this sentence, word for word, to at least three other women, did not prevent him, as he said it, from sincerely believing it to be the truth.

'But I feel terrified too,' he went on, 'that you'll decide to give me up after all and marry Michael instead. Remember, I shall never blame you in the least if you do. It would probably be much more sensible. But to me you are the only woman—'

At this juncture the duchess opened the linen cupboard door and popped her head round the corner.

'Oh, you darlings,' she said delightedly, 'I'm so glad somebody's having a lovely time. It does me good to see you. You've no idea what it's been like everywhere else, too

172

gloomy and awful for words. Now, when you've quite finished being happy together in there we've got some cocktails in Bobby's room, so mind you come along and join us.'

She shut the door carefully and went, bursting with her news, back to Bobby.

'There they were, *locked* in each other's arms. I can't tell you how sweet they looked—the lambs. Quite frankly, I never should have thought Philadelphia had so much sense. I must ask her to stay as soon as ever we get back from Switzerland.'

'Now don't you start encouraging her,' said Bobby crossly. 'Amabelle and I are working like niggers to stop all this nonsense and make her get engaged to Michael.'

'Oh, *no*, you awful child, you can't behave like a match-making mamma at your age; it's not natural. For heaven's sake let the poor girl have her fun, besides, it's so good for her. Just think how pretty she's looking now. She is a different being from what she was a month ago.'

'I'm all in favour of her having as much fun as she likes,' said Bobby, 'so long as she'll be sensible and not go on with all this ridiculous talk about marriage—just think, if Michael heard about it, he might quite easily be put off for good.'

'You don't seriously want her to marry Michael, do you? He's such a fearful bore. I wouldn't allow a daughter of mine to marry him, however much she wanted to.'

'That's just very silly and naughty of you, darling Auntie Loudie, because a girl's first husband must be eligible, otherwise she will very soon go downhill altogether. Amabelle agrees with me.'

'Amabelle is so frightfully pompous in these days,' said the duchess with a hiccough. 'I can remember the time when she was just an ordinary tart (a very successful one and all that, of course) and then she really was the greatest fun. We used to go secretly to her parties and think we were being absolute dare-devils, but ever since she married old James Fortescue she's been twice as much of a duchess as I am. It's a great pity, because in those days she used to be too heavenly.'

'I think she is still,' said Bobby stoutly. 'She's one of the sweetest people in the world. Look how divine she has been to the Monteaths ever since that baby was born.'

'Yes, I agree she is very sweet and kind, she always has been. I'm only saying that she's no longer such absolutely rollicking fun. In any case, I think it's absurd for her to take that line about Delphie. Why surely the child is rich enough to marry anybody she likes.'

'She's only rich so long as my mother chooses to make her an allowance.'

'Clearly. But I suppose that even darling Gloria could hardly see her own daughter starve. I don't understand what there is against Paul myself. He seems an exceptionally nice young man, good-looking, polite, everything one could want for a son-in-law.'

'Well, to begin with, if you'd really like to know, his name isn't Fisher at all.'

'Oh?'

'It's Fotheringay, Paul Fotheringay.'

'My dear, that's a much nicer name than Fisher. Most romantic, too. One of Henry VIII's wives was executed at a place called that. I remember all about it in English history.'

'Darling, I don't think you quite understand. His real name, as I said before, is Paul Fotheringay, and he is masquerading here under the alias of Fisher.'

'How divinely thrilling. Wait a moment, though, wasn't there somebody called Paul Fotheringay who wrote that screamingly funny book about pawnbrokers trying to commit suicide?'

'Yes, that's his book, *Crazy Capers*.'

'Oh, but I've never laughed so much at anything before in my life. Wait a minute while I rush to the linen cupboard— it's too bad, I haven't my copy here for him to autograph. It *was* a heavenly book. Bobby, you little monster, why ever didn't you tell me this before?'

'You see he's here in disguise really,' said Bobby, unbending a little, 'because he wants to write the life of Lady Maria. He asked mother in a letter whether he could borrow

174

the journal, and she wrote back awfully rudely, so then he got taken on as my tutor and ever since then he has been studying it for his book.'

'Well I should think that will be a scream,' said the duchess. 'Delphie will be mad if she doesn't marry him, but if she doesn't I shall, that's all. What I do adore is a really good sense of humour. The funny thing is that though I've liked Paul from the very beginning he never struck me as being so particularly amusing, but of course that must have been entirely my own fault. Shake up one more cocktail, won't you, Bobby, my sweet—here's Héloïse back again. Dear, what a pudding-faced young man she has got with her this time. Where can she have picked him up? Héloïse, what do you think, Philadelphia and Paul have been sitting out for more than two hours in the linen cupboard.'

'Oh, where—can I see?'

'No, certainly you can't. It's nothing whatever to do with you. I may say I'm surprised you've not been in there yourself.'

'If Maydew had come I don't doubt I should have been,' said Héloïse, 'but all the young men here seem to be so sexless. I honestly don't think I've ever been to such an awful party as this in my life. Can I introduce Mr. Wainscote to you, by the way. He has been to a lot of jolly shows lately in London, and I expect he'd like a cocktail, Bobby.'

'As a matter of fact,' said Mr. Wainscote, blushing, 'the rest of my party is very anxious to go home—I mean,' he added hurriedly, looking at Bobby, 'ready to leave. We have all enjoyed ourselves immensely, but we have a long cold drive before us, so I think that perhaps I should say good-bye,' and he edged out of the room sideways like a crab.

'My darling Hèloïse, what an extraordinary young man,' said the duchess.

'He's not at all extraordinary,' said Héloïse, 'unless you mean extraordinarily attractive. I'm rather in love with him myself,' and she looked under long blue eyelashes at Bobby.

'No cop, old girl, you can't lead me on like that. I know you're in a temper because I haven't spoken to you the whole evening, but there's no point in making a fool of yourself just the same. Have another cegocktegail?'

'I degon't megind egif egI dego,' said Héloïse, happily settling herself on the edge of the bed. 'Now run along downstairs, mother, if you don't mind, because I want to kiss Bobby.'

'All right, I'll go and see how Rosemary and Laetitia are getting on. Have a lovely time, and don't be too long.'

Shortly after this, Bobby himself came downstairs, and revolted by the sights and sounds of cheerlessness which greeted his eyes, thoughtfully turned out the electric light at the main, thus breaking up the party. By the flickering rays of the only candle that Compton Bobbin possessed, coats were found, adieux were said, and, grumbling to the last, the flower of Gloucestershire man and maidenhood climbed into their Morris Cowleys and drove away.

This contretemps postponed but did not avert Lady Bobbin's furious upbraiding of Bobby and Philadelphia, who, having disappeared at the first dance on the programme, had never been seen again mingling with their guests.

'I know it's all Louisa's fault,' she said angrily, 'and I'm damned if I'll go on having that woman to the house. I'm sick and tired of her rudeness, and as for that little—Héloïse, I'd much sooner neither of you had any more to do with her.'

Paul and Philadelphia parted the next day with tears and promises of eternal fidelity. Their farewells were rendered slightly more bearable than they would otherwise have been by the fact that Aunt Loudie, having given them the only moral support they had as yet received, had promised that she would invite Philadelphia to stay in London as soon as she herself should return from Switzerland.

'See you very soon, my darling,' said Paul, as they stood on Woodford platform waiting for his train.

'Yes, darling. And mind you write to me.'

'Of course I will, every day. And mind you do, too. Take care of yourself, my precious, and don't worry too much. Everything will come all right in the end, you'll see.'

'I don't know,' said Philadelphia, miserably.

'Now come on,' said Bobby impatiently as the train came to a standstill, 'jump in, Paul—good-bye, Delphie, come and see me at Eton some time, old girl. Don't let them forget to send on my letters and parcels. Good-bye—good-bye.'

To Philadelphia, left alone on the cold, wet and empty platform, it seemed as though all happiness had come to an end. She cried so much that she could hardly see to drive her car home.

Paul and Bobby lounged luxuriously in their first-class carriage (it was one of Bobby's talents that he could always travel first-class on a third-class ticket), and argued as to whether they should lunch at the Ritz or the Berkeley, and what film they should go to afterwards. At Oxford they got out and bought all the illustrated papers. Paul felt agreeably sentimental and wretched, but he was glad, on the whole, to be going back to London. The only drawback was that he had promised Philadelphia to look for work, a pastime that he detested, and worse still, to do work if he found it. Much would he have preferred to settle down in a desultory manner to his life of Lady Maria Bobbin. However, he put these unpleasant thoughts from him without any difficulty and was soon deep in perusal of *The Tatler*.

Philadelphia wandered about Compton Bobbin like a lost soul. She could find no comfort in her situation. It was typical, she thought again, of the malignant spirit which apparently controlled her destiny to cram just one month of her life with fascinating people and events, only to remove them all in a single day, leaving in their place a few memories to make everything seem flatter, more dreary than before. Paul had gone, Sally and Walter had gone for ever, Amabelle would not, it appeared, be back before Easter—her plans for a country wedding had been altered; she now intended to get married quietly in London as soon as the lambing season should be over and go to her villa on the Riviera for the honeymoon.

Philadelphia found herself once more without any occupation or interests, and for the rest of that day she sat before

177

the fire in an arm-chair, assailed by the ghastly boredom only known to those who live in the country but have no love for country pursuits, and no intellectual resources on which they can fall back. And in the clutches of that boredom, too boring even to describe, she remained during the weeks to come. She would get up in the morning as late as she dared, and read the papers over and over again, hoping to pass the time until luncheon. In the afternoon she would go for a little walk, and when she came in from that would sit or wander aimlessly about the house, waiting for tea. After tea she would perhaps try to read some improving work suggested to her by Michael, or, more often, play canfield on the schoolroom table (if this comes out it means that he loves me and I shall marry him) until it was time to have her bath and change for dinner. The evenings were occupied with wireless, to which Lady Bobbin was devoted. And so the days dragged on, from one meal to the next. Poor Philadelphia hardly employed the best methods with which to fight depression, but it is difficult to know, under the circumstances, what else she could have done. Her education had not fitted her for study, and in any case, like most women, she was only really interested in personalities. When she received a letter from Paul it would colour a whole day, and she would spend hours reading, re-reading and answering it; but he wrote at the most irregular intervals. Like most people who write for a living he hated writing letters, and moreover seldom had any notepaper in his lodgings.

Michael, on the other hand, wrote from his bed of jaundice nearly every day. Although his letters were, in tone, more those of a father than a lover, he evidently quite regarded himself as engaged to Philadelphia, and she was too indolent, and too much afraid of bringing matters to a climax to disillusion him. Besides, she rather enjoyed receiving and answering his letters. Lady Bobbin also assumed that the engagement was to be announced as soon as Michael recovered.

Meanwhile, Paul was leading his usual happy-go-lucky existence in London. He obtained, without much difficulty, a 'job' in his uncle's office. The uncle having flatly refused to give him work, was quite glad to let him sit for a few hours every day in the office, at a pound a week, so that he might obtain that background of respectability which was to prove such a valuable factor in influencing Lady Bobbin. He still loved Philadelphia very much, and wanted nothing more than to marry her, but he felt that since several months must now elapse before it would be in any way feasible to ask her mother's consent, he might as well pass those months as pleasantly as he could. With this end in view he went, a few days after his arrival in London, to a fancy-dress party given in a tiny flat off the Brompton Road. On entering the room, which was a seething mass of travesty, the togas of ancient Rome and the beards of Elizabethan England rubbing against the talc wings of modern fairyland, he was immediately greeted with cries of enthusiasm by Marcella Bracket.

'Here's darling Paul. Oh, how cross I am with you. Where have you been all this time? I've done nothing but ring you up for weeks. You might have sent me a Christmas card, you ogre.'

Paul tried to ignore the girl, he really tried hard. Nevertheless, before the night was over he had abjectly apologized for his neglect of her during the past month, and had finally found himself with her in his arms, her large painted mouth pressed to his as of yore.

The next day he woke up with a bad headache and a worse conscience.

'This is really terrible,' he thought, 'I must pull myself together. How can I, how can I be behaving in this caddish manner whilst poor little Philadelphia is shut up in that dreary house with no one to speak to but Lady Bobbin, and she out hunting all day. It is beginning to look as if Amabelle were right in saying that I have no talent for true love. I am evidently incapable of being faithful to one person. All the same, I do love Philadelphia far, far the best, although Marcella seems to have this extraordinary effect on me.'

And he resolved never to see Marcella again. That

determined young woman, however, was not easily to be put off. She had just suffered a serious reverse in her own love affairs, and it suited her very well to have Paul hanging around her once more. Paul, on the other hand, lonely, worried and very much attracted by Marcella, did not require a great deal of encouragement, and at the end of a fortnight they were inseparable.

21

As soon as Michael was allowed to move again he returned by train to Compton Bobbin to arrange about his wedding. No doubts whatever had crossed his mind as to Philadelphia's attitude towards him, and he travelled as far as London with perfect serenity. On his way through London he took the opportunity to lunch with Amabelle, and she immediately put him in possession of all the facts with regard to Paul and Philadelphia, once more giving it as her opinion that the whole affair was a piece of childish nonsense.

'Everything will be quite all right,' she said, 'if you do as I tell you. First of all, you'd better go round to Cartier this afternoon and buy her a lovely ring and some other little present as well, one of those diamond bracelets for instance. I should give her the bracelet when you arrive, but keep the ring for a day or two to give her when she has been really nice to you—it will seem more romantic like that. Be very sweet and sympathetic, of course, but perfectly firm, make her feel she is definitely engaged to you; and if by any chance she should mention Paul, take up the attitude of being surprised and pained but ready to forgive just this once. I should try to keep off the subject for as long as you can, though. I think you will find that, what with the boredom of her present existence and her fear of you (she regards you with a good deal of wholesome awe, you know), she will be beside you on the altar steps in no time. That's what you really do want, I suppose?'

'Yes, yes,' said Michael, adding uncertainly: 'Poor child, I only hope I shall be able to make her happy. You know, Amabelle, that it is you who will always be the love of my life, don't you?'

'Nonsense, my dear, of course you'll make her happy. You two are cut out for each other, obviously. As for Paul, I'm very fond of him myself, but all the same I feel perfectly certain that she would be wretched with him; he has far too weak a character to marry a girl of her sort. He needs something really hard-boiled. Why, at this very moment he is having an affair with that awful Marcella Bracket, whom he actually dislikes—I've no patience with him sometimes, I must say.'

Michael looked very much relieved. 'Then he's not in love with Philadelphia at all?'

'I tell you the whole thing is nonsense from beginning to end, and it's the greatest mercy that you are about again and can put a stop to it. All the same, I believe that in his queer way he does love Philadelphia, only he hasn't the strength of mind to get rid of the Bracket. Now, Michael dear, you must be off. My last words to you are to be firm and don't forget the diamond bracelet. It ought to work wonders for you.'

Michael followed this advice to the letter. Immediately on leaving Portman Square, he went to Cartier, where he bought a large and beautiful emerald ring and a diamond bracelet of magnificent proportions. With these in his pocket he caught the 4·45 from Paddington, arriving at Compton Bobbin just in time to dress for dinner.

He was met by his Aunt Gloria with the news that Philadelphia had gone to bed with a headache.

'In that case,' he said, 'I think I will go up and see her for a moment,' and before Lady Bobbin, gratified but somewhat scandalized at such haste, had time to utter a half-hearted protest, he had run up the stairs and was knocking at Philadelphia's bedroom door.

It would be idle to pretend that Philadelphia was not pleased to see him. The boredom and depression of the last few weeks had been such that she was ready to welcome with delight any new face, anybody from the outer world. With the greatest reluctance she had forced herself to avoid him by pretending to be ill, feeling in some obscure way that loyalty to Paul demanded this gesture, and when Michael came up to see her immediately on his arrival she was more touched and pleased than she cared to admit.

He sat on the edge of her bed and talked of this and that, cheerfully and without embarrassment, looking most attractively pale and thin from his recent illness. Presently, having made no mention whatever of an engagement, he said: 'Now I must have my bath, or I shall be late for Aunt Gloria, and you ought to go to sleep if you're not very well, so I will say good night. But first of all put out your hand and shut your eyes, darling.' Philadelphia did so, and he snapped the diamond bracelet on to her wrist.

The diamond is a stone possessed for the female mind, however unsophisticated, of curious psychological attributes. Philadelphia looked at the sparkling flowers on her wrist and forgot that she had been about to announce her betrothal to another. She flung her arms around Michael's neck in an access of childlike pleasure and cried: 'Oh, the lovely bracelet. Thank you, thank you, darling Michael. You are sweet to me.'

Amabelle's love potion had done its work for the moment. Its effect, however, wore off sadly during the night, and the next morning, very early, at about six o'clock, Philadelphia woke up tormented with agonies of self-reproach.

'Paul, my darling, darling Paul,' she wept into her pillow. 'I won't lose you; they shan't bribe me like this. I will never give you up, never, as long as I live.' She flung the offending bracelet, which gleamed beneath her bedside lamp, into the farthest corner of the room, sobbing bitterly. After a while she pulled herself together and began to consider her position. The idea had come to her that if she should stay any longer at Compton Bobbin now that Michael had arrived, she would inevitably find herself engaged to him. She knew that she was too weak to offer, alone and unsupported, any real resistance; and she dreaded beyond words the idea of those frightful scenes with her mother which would certainly ensue if she did. If she was ever to escape, now and now only, was the time. It would be her last opportunity. She must go, at once, to Paul.

Having taken this decision she began very quickly to dress. Better leave the house before anybody was about. She slipped

183

downstairs, feeling like an escaping criminal, took the key of
the garage from the hall table, climbed out of the school-room
window into the cold, dark morning air, and by seven o'clock
was well on the road to London in her little car. She would be
in time to have breakfast with Paul before he left for his office.
Poor darling, how he must hate working in such a place; it
was wonderful to think of him doing it for her sake.
Everything would be all right when she was with him, and she
would be safe again. The idea of seeing him so soon filled her
with nervous excitement.

Shortly after nine o'clock she drove up to the house in
Ebury Street where Paul had rooms. Her heart beat in great
thumps as she rang the front door bell. For an eternity there
was no answer; at last, however, the door was opened by an
elderly woman who held in one hand a bucket of soapy water.
She looked at Philadelphia with hostility and said, in reply to
her question. 'Mr. Fotheringay has not been called yet.'
Philadelphia hesitated. She felt cold and dazed after her long
drive.

'I must see him, though,' she said at last. 'It is very
important. I am his sister. Please will you show me the way to
his room?'

The woman shrugged her shoulders. 'Mr. Fotheringay is
on the first floor, but he gave orders that he was not to be
called. You must please yourself,' she said, and falling to her
knees she began scrubbing the linoleum on the floor.

Philadelphia went upstairs timidly. She knocked several
times on the first door that she came to, and finally, receiving
no answer, she turned the handle and walked in. The room
was evidently a sitting-room, and at first sight seemed to be
empty, although the electric light was burning. Suddenly,
however, it was empty no more, for she realized with a start
that Paul himself lay on the sofa, fully dressed.

In certain emergencies the human brain neglects to register
such subsidiary emotions as that of surprise. To Philadelphia,
overstrung, hysterical, and worn out by her long and fasting
drive, it seemed quite natural that Paul should be lying on his
sofa instead of in his bed, that he should still be wearing

evening dress at nine o'clock in the morning, and that although he was fast asleep the electric light should be turned on, shining full in his face. A person of more experience might have been prepared for what followed; Philadelphia only felt an overpowering relief that she had found him again. Everything must be all right now, it seemed.

'Paul,' she said, leaning over him. 'Darling. Wake up.'

No answer. No movement. No sound in the room but that of his thick, heavy and regular breathing. She touched him rather shyly on the arm. 'Please wake up, Paul.' She shook him gently. She shook him really hard. 'Paul, don't be so unkind to me. You must wake up. I've come so far to see you. Please, please, my darling.'

At last he half-opened his eyes, looked at her as though from a great distance, and said in a thick voice: 'For God's sake, leave me alone. I told them not to call me,' after which he turned over deliberately and once more lay motionless.

'Paul, you must speak to me,' she cried, shaking now with angry sobs, and losing all self-control she began to hit him on the chest until he opened his eyes again. This time he seemed to recognize her. He took one of her hands in his and said with a great effort, 'Go away, darling, I'm drunk.' After that neither tears nor protestations could move him.

Philadelphia went slowly down the stairs. That was the end. She must get back to Michael, who would never treat her so. She felt sick and faint now, and was blinded by her tears. The woman who had let her in was scrubbing the front door steps. Philadelphia passed her quickly, aware of curious looks, got into her car and drove down the street until she thought she must be out of sight. Then, oblivious of passers-by, she stopped and cried until she could cry no more. After that she began to think of what she should do next. In spite of her unhappiness she realized that to drive home at once in her present condition would be impossible; she must have something to eat first, and a rest. Whom did she know in London? Her Aunt Loudie was in Switzerland, Sally was almost certainly still on the Riviera. Amabelle—she would be kind. She started up the engine of the car and, after getting

185

lost several times, for she did not know her way about London, she found herself at last outside Amabelle's house. She rang the front door bell; there was no answer. She rang again, and presently a red-faced footman appeared still struggling into his coat.

'Can I see Mrs. Fortescue, please?'

'Mrs. Fortescue has not been called yet.'

Philadelphia was trying to decide what she should say next when she found that the door had been rudely shut in her face. Such terrible things had happened to her already that this incident, which on any ordinary occasion would have caused her unspeakable mortification, seemed quite unimportant. She even sat in her car this time without bothering to move on while she considered what her next step should be. Sally was her last remaining hope, if she was back from the Riviera all would be well. She drove to Fitzroy Square. 'Please, God, let her be there please, please.' This time the door was opened immediately by a fat and smiling charlady.

'Yes, Mrs. Monteath came back last night. Will you come this way, please.'

'Thank you, God, thank you, thank you.'

She took Philadelphia up to the first floor flat, opened the door of it with a special key and precipitated her into a large, light bedroom, where Sally and Walter Monteath were sitting up in bed eating their breakfast.

'A young lady to see you, ma'am.'

'Philadelphia darling!' cried Sally in a loud and cheerful voice.

Philadelphia opened her mouth to say something and then fell to the floor in a dead faint.

When she recovered consciousness she was lying in the bed herself, and Sally was sponging her face with cold water while the charwoman looked on. Walter was nowhere to be seen.

'There, darling,' said Sally, 'you lie quite still and don't worry about anything.'

'I'm so sorry,' said Philadelphia, 'to be such a bother.'

'Don't be silly. Are you feeling all right now?'

186

'Yes, perfect. I expect I'm rather hungry really, that's why I fainted.'

'Poor sweet. Mrs. Crumpit will make you some breakfast at once. You didn't motor all the way up this morning, did you?'

'Yes, I did.'

'Good gracious. Walter thought you had by the look of the car.'

Philadelphia felt warm, happy and contented. She was in no hurry to tell her story, and Sally did not ask any more questions, but went off to help Mrs. Crumpit in the kitchen. Presently she came back with a most delicious breakfast. While Philadelphia was eating this the telephone bell rang in the next room and Walter's voice could be heard answering it.

'Hullo—yes? Oh, hullo, Amabelle—my dear, she's in our bed, quite all right—she appeared about half-an-hour ago and fainted away. Gave us an awful fright, but she's eating breakfast now. What? I don't know. I've no idea. Oh, very well, we'll keep her for the present then. Right you are, Amabelle. Good-bye.'

'You seem to have caused a perfect uproar,' he said, coming into the bedroom. 'Apparently Michael had been telephoning to Amabelle from Compton Bobbin half out of his mind, and she tried to get on to Paul, but there was no answer; and then by a stroke of luck it occurred to her that we might know something about you. Michael is on his way to London now. I must go and have my bath. See you later.'

'Do tell me all about it,' said Sally as he shut the door. 'I'm eaten with curiosity.'

'Well, you see, Michael arrived at home last night and gave me a diamond bracelet.'

'Darling, how gorgeous.'

'And I simply hadn't the courage to tell him about Paul. I couldn't face the scene with mother; you don't know how terrifying she can be. But I thought that if I went to Paul straight away everything would be all right. I thought it was my only chance. So I got up very early this morning—'

'You must have.'

'And drove up here and went straight to Paul's house, and when I got there,' she said, her voice shaking, 'he was lying on the sofa looking too awful, and he wouldn't speak to me or even bother to open his eyes.'

'Blind, I suppose,' said Sally with the wisdom of experience.

'Yes, he was. At last when I had shaken him for ages all he said was, "Go away—I'm drunk." Sally, I never knew people got drunk in the morning?'

'I expect he had a jolly old hangover,' said Sally. 'What did you do then?'

'As soon as I realized what was the matter I went to Amabelle's, because I thought you were still abroad, but she hadn't been called and the footman was rude to me, so I came here on the chance that I might find you.'

'You've been crying, haven't you?'

'Well, of course. It's so terrible to think that all this time I've been in love with a drunkard.'

'Paul's not a drunkard, my dear; that's absurd. All men get blind sometimes, but they don't expect their girl friends to call at nine in the morning as a rule.'

'Anyway, it's all over between us now. I couldn't bear to see him again after that.'

'Couldn't you?'

'Never. It was too horrible. He could never have done such a thing if he had really loved me. Michael couldn't behave like that; he does love me, I know, and I shall be frightfully happy with him now.'

'I never doubted that you would be happy with Michael,' said Sally in a dry voice. 'For one thing, you weren't at any time properly in love with Paul. He was the first person who had ever made love to you and you fell for him; but that doesn't count.'

'Oh, Sally, you don't understand. I adored him right up to this morning more than anybody in the world. You couldn't go on being in love with somebody after a thing like that had happened, could you?'

'But of course you could. That sort of thing doesn't make a

scrap of difference if you really love somebody. When I think of all the times I've put Walter to bed absolutely paralytic with drink! You weren't a bit in love with Paul, my sweet, and you've realized it, that's all. And I think it's a mercy you have, myself, because you are entirely unsuited to each other in every way. You would both have been miserably unhappy. Now, you'll be able to marry that divine Michael and have a really enviable life. Don't cry, darling, but have some more coffee and then I'll lend you some rouge. You mustn't be looking pale for Michael when he comes.'

Two days later Paul read in *The Times* that a marriage had been arranged and would shortly take place between the Marquis of Lewes and Philadelphia, only daughter of Lady Bobbin and the late Sir Hudson Bobbin, of Compton Bobbin, Gloucestershire.

With a sigh, whether of sadness or relief will never be known, he settled down to write the first chapter of his *Life and Works of Lady Maria Bobbin.*

FINE WORKS OF FICTION AND NON-FICTION AVAILABLE FROM CARROLL & GRAF

☐ Asch, Sholem/EAST RIVER $3.95
☐ Brown, Harry/A WALK IN THE SUN $3.95
☐ Chester, Alfred/THE EXQUISITE CORPSE $4.95
☐ Burnett, W. R./HIGH SIERRA $3.50
☐ Cozzens, James Gould/THE LAST ADAM $4.95
☐ Crichton, Robert/THE CAMERONS $4.95
☐ Crichton, Robert/THE SECRET OF SANTA
    VITTORIA $3.95
☐ De Quincey, Thomas/CONFESSIONS OF AN
    ENGLISH OPIUM EATER AND OTHER
    WRITINGS $4.95
☐ Farrell, J.G./TROUBLES $4.95
☐ Farrell, J.G./THE SIEGE OF KRISHNAPUR $4.95
☐ Farrell, J.G./THE SINGAPORE GRIP $4.95
☐ Garbus, Martin/READY FOR THE DEFENSE $4.95
☐ Gresham, William Lindsay/NIGHTMARE ALLEY $3.50
☐ Gurney, Jr., A.R./THE SNOW BALL $4.50
☐ Higgins, George V./A CHOICE OF ENEMIES $3.50
☐ Higgins, George V./COGAN'S TRADE $3.50
☐ Higgins, George V./PENANCE FOR JERRY
    KENNEDY $3.50
☐ Hilton, James/RANDOM HARVEST $4.50
☐ Huxley, Aldous/GREY EMINENCE $4.95
☐ Innes, Hammond/THE NAKED LAND $3.50
☐ Innes, Hammond/ATLANTIC FURY $3.50
☐ Innes, Hammond/SOLOMON'S SEAL $3.50
☐ Innes, Hammond/THE WRECK OF THE MARY
    DEARE $3.50
☐ Johnson, Josephine/NOW IN NOVEMBER $4.50
☐ Kipling, Rudyard/THE LIGHT THAT FAILED $3.95
☐ L'Amour, Louis/LAW OF THE DESERT BORN $2.95
☐ Lewis, Norman/THE SICILIAN SPECIALIST $3.50

☐	Lewis, Norman/THE MAN IN THE MIDDLE	$3.50
☐	Mason, A.E.W./THE FOUR FEATHERS	$3.95
☐	Martin, David/FINAL HARBOR	$4.95
☐	Masters, John/THEOPHILUS NORTH	$4.95
☐	Masters, John/BHOWANI JUNCTION	$4.50
☐	Mitford, Nancy/PIGEON PIE	$3.95
☐	Mitford, Nancy/CHRISTMAS PUDDING	$3.95
☐	O'Hara, John/FROM THE TERRACE	$4.95
☐	O'Hara, John/SERMONS AND SODA WATER	$4.95
☐	O'Hara, John/HOPE OF HEAVEN	$3.95
☐	O'Hara, John/A RAGE TO LIVE	$4.95
☐	O'Hara, John/TEN NORTH FREDERICK	$4.50
☐	Proffitt, Nicholas/GARDENS OF STONE	$4.50
☐	Purdy, James/CABOT WRIGHT BEGINS	$4.50
☐	Rechy, John/BODIES AND SOULS	$4.50
☐	Reilly, Sidney/BRITAIN'S GREATEST SPY	$3.95
☐	Scott, Paul/THE LOVE PAVILION	$4.50
☐	Scott, Paul/THE CORRIDA AT SAN FELIU	$3.95
☐	Scott, Paul/A MALE CHILD	$3.95
☐	Short, Luke/MARSHAL OF VENGEANCE	$2.95
☐	Smith, Joseph/THE DAY THE MUSIC DIED	$4.95
☐	Taylor, Peter/IN THE MIRO DISTRICT	$3.95
☐	Thirkell, Angela/THE BRANDONS	$4.95
☐	Thirkell, Angela/POMFRET TOWERS	$4.95
☐	Wharton, William/SCUMBLER	$3.95
☐	Wilder, Thornton/THE EIGTH DAY	$4.95
☐	Wilder, Thornton/THE CABALA	$3.95

Available from fine bookstores everywhere or use this coupon for ordering: